A Practical N

John Davidson

Alpha Editions

This edition published in 2024

ISBN 9789361471520

Design and Setting By

Alpha Editions
www.alphaedis.com

Email - info@alphaedis.com

As per information held with us this book is in Public Domain.
This book is a reproduction of an important historical work.
Alpha Editions uses the best technology to reproduce historical work
in the same manner it was first published to preserve its original nature.
Any marks or number seen are left intentionally to preserve.

Contents

CHAPTER I	- 1 -
CHAPTER II	- 8 -
CHAPTER III	- 17 -
CHAPTER IV	- 20 -
CHAPTER V	- 25 -
CHAPTER VI	- 35 -
CHAPTER VII	- 40 -
CHAPTER VIII	- 46 -
CHAPTER IX	- 49 -
CHAPTER X	- 56 -
CHAPTER XI	- 62 -

CHAPTER I

BAGGING A HERO

'WELL, but the novel is played out, Carry. It has run to seed. Anybody can get the seed; anybody can sow it. If it goes on at this rate, novel-writers will soon be in a majority, and novel-reading will become a lucrative employment.'

'What are you going to do, then, Maxwell? Here's Peter out of work, and my stitching can't support three.'

The three in question were Maxwell Lee, his wife Caroline, and her brother, Peter Briscoe. Lee was an unsuccessful literary man; his brother-in-law, Briscoe, an unsuccessful business-man. Caroline, on the other hand, was entirely successful in an arduous endeavour to be a man, hoping and working for all three.

We have nothing whatever to do with the past of these people. We start with the conversation introduced in the first sentence. Caroline had urged on Lee the advisability of accepting an offer from the editor of a country weekly. But Lee, who had composed dramas and philosophical romances which no publisher, nor editor could be got to read, refused scornfully the task of writing an 'ordinary, vulgar, sentimental and sensational story of the kind required.'

'What am I going to do?' he said. 'I'll tell you: I am going to create a novel. Practical joking is the new novel in its infancy. The end of every thought is an action; and the centuries of written fiction must culminate in an age of acted fiction. We stand upon the threshold of that age, and I am destined to open the door.'

Caroline sighed, and Briscoe shot out his underlip: evidence that they were accustomed to this sort of thing.

Lee continued: 'You shall collaborate with me in the production of this novel. Think of it! Novel-writing is effete; novel-creation is about to begin. We shall cause a novel to take place in the world. We shall construct a plot; we shall select a hero; we shall enter into his life, and produce the series of events before determined on. Consider for a minute. We can do nothing else now. The last development, the naturalist school, is a mere copying, a bare photographing of life—at least, that is what it professes to be. This is not art. There can never be an art of novel-writing. But there can be—there shall be, you will aid me to begin the art of novel-creation.'

'Do you propose to make a living by it?' inquired Briscoe.

'Certainly.'

Briscoe rose, and without comment left the house. Caroline looked at her husband with a glance of mingled pity and amusement.

'Why are you so fantastic?' she asked softly.

'You laugh at my idea now, because you do not see it as I see it. Wait till it is completely developed before you condemn it.'

Caroline made no reply; but went on with her sewing. Lee threw himself at full length on a rickety sofa and closed his eyes. Besides the sofa, two chairs and a table, a rag of carpet before the fire-place, a shelf with some books of poetry and novels, and an old oil-painting in a dark corner, made up the furniture of the room. There were three other apartments, a kitchen and two bedrooms, all as scantily furnished. The house was in the top flat of a four-storey land in Peyton Street, Glasgow.

Lee dozed and dreamed. Caroline sewed steadily. An hour elapsed without a word from either. Then both were aroused by the noisy entrance of Briscoe, who, having let himself into the house by his latch-key, strode into the parlour with a portmanteau in either hand. He thrashed these down on the floor with defiant emphasis, and said, frowning away a grin: 'Your twin-brother's traps, Lee. I'll bring *him* upstairs, too.'

He went out immediately, as if afraid of being recalled.

'Your twin-brother!' exclaimed Mrs. Lee. 'I never heard of him.'

'And I hear of him for the first time.'

They waited in amazement the return of Briscoe. Soon an irregular and shuffling tread sounded from the stair; and in a minute he and a cabman entered the parlour, bearing between them what seemed the lifeless body of a man. This they placed on the sofa. The cabman looked about him curiously; but, being apparently satisfied with his fare, withdrew.

When he was gone, Briscoe spoke: 'This is the first chapter of your novel, Lee. Something startling to begin with, eh?'

'What do you mean?'

'I've bagged a hero for you.'

'Bagged a hero!'

'Yes; kidnapped a millionaire in the middle of Glasgow in broad daylight. Here's how it happened: one instant I saw a man with his head out of a cab-window, shouting to the driver; the next, the cab-door, which can't have been properly fastened, sprang open, and the man was lying in the street. On going up to him, I said to myself, "Maxwell Lee, as I'm a sinner!" You're wonderfully like, even when I look at your faces alternately. Well, I shouted in his ear, "Chartres! Chartres!" seeing his name in his hat which had fallen off, and pretending to know him perfectly. I felt so mad at you and your absurd notions of creating novels, that, without thinking of the consequences, I got him into the cab again, told the policeman that he was my brother-in-law, and drove straight here. It was all done so suddenly, and I assumed such confidence, that the police did not so much as demand my address. Of course, if you don't want to have anything to do with him, I suppose we can make it out a case of mistaken identity.'

'Who is he, I wonder?' said Lee, whose eyes were sparkling.

'There's his name and address,' replied Briscoe, pointing to the portmanteaus.

Lee read aloud: '"Mr. Henry Chartres, Snell House, Gourock, N.B."' He then pressed his head in both hands, knit his brows, tightened his mouth, and regarded the floor for fully a minute.

As soon as Chartres had been laid on the sofa, Caroline wiped the mud from his face and hands. There was not a cushion in the room, but she brought two pillows from her own bed, and with them propped the head and shoulders of the unconscious man. While Lee was still contemplating the floor, she said, 'We must get a doctor at once.'

Lee's response was a muttered 'Yes, yes;' but the question brought him nearer the facts of the case than he had been since Briscoe explained his motive in possessing himself of Mr. Chartres.

'A doctor!' repeated Caroline.

'Of course, of course,' said Lee, approaching the sofa for the first time. He studied the still unconscious face while Caroline and Briscoe watched him: the first wondering that he should seem to hesitate to send for a doctor, and the other with an incredulous curiosity. Briscoe, an ill-natured, half-educated man, had been seized by a sudden inspiration on seeing the likeness between Chartres and his brother-in-law. He thought to overset Lee's new idea by showing him its impracticability. He believed that failure had unhinged his brother-in-law's mind; and knew for certain that no argument could possibly avail. He trusted that by introducing Chartres under such extraordinary circumstances into what he regarded as Lee's insane waking dream the gross absurdity of it—absurd at least in his impecunious state—would become apparent to him. Having once unfixed this idea, he hoped, with the help of Mrs. Lee, to force his acceptance of the commission for the country weekly. The result was not going to be what he expected. Lee was taking his brother's collaboration seriously. A childish smile of wonder and delight overspread his features, as his likeness to Chartres appeared more fully, in his estimation, upon a detailed examination. He got a looking-glass, and compared the two faces, placing the mirror so that the reflection of his lay as if he had rested his head on Chartres' shoulder. Thick, soft, grey hair, inclined still to curl, and divided on the left side; a broad forehead, perpendicular for an inch above the eyebrows, then sloping inordinately to the beginning of the hair; eyebrows distinctly marked, but not heavy; a well-formed nose, rather long, and approaching the aquiline; full, curved lips; the mouth not small, but liker a woman's than a man's; the chin, almost feminine, little and rounded; the cheeks smooth, and the face clean shaved. There was no doubt that the men might have been twins, and that their most intimate associates would have been constantly mistaking them.

'It's wonderful—wonderful, Peter!' said Lee. 'What a brilliant stroke of yours this is!'

'But the doctor, Maxwell!' cried Caroline, who was becoming impatient.

'Perhaps we'll not need one,' replied her husband. 'See, he's coming round!'

Chartres began to move uneasily; the blood dawned in his cheeks; and his breathing grew more vigorous. He opened his eyes and attempted to raise his head; but a twinge of pain forced a groan from him, and he again fainted.

'We must get him into bed, in the first place,' said Lee.

With much difficulty this was accomplished. Then Caroline renewed her demand for a doctor; but her husband, professing to have some skill in medicine, declared himself able to treat Chartres, who seemed to have fallen on the top of his head. Cold water, he assured his wife, would soon remove the effects of the concussion. Briscoe also said that there was no need for a doctor. Mrs. Lee did not feel called on to dispute the point; and was about to resume the cold applications, when it struck her, for the first, how very extraordinary a thing it was that this stranger should be in their house.

'Why is he here?' she cried. 'What are you going to do with him?'

'We are going to make use of him in our story, my dear,' said Lee, mildly. 'We will not do him any harm, but we may keep him prisoner here for a little.'

'How cruel! Besides, it would be a crime,' remonstrated his wife.

Lee answered very calmly, but with a consuming fire in his eyes:

'We'll not be cruel if we can possibly help it; and, as for its being criminal, surely no novel is complete without a crime. At the start of this new departure in the art of fiction we will be much hampered in its exercise by scruples and fears of this kind. Some of us may even require to be martyrs. For example: should it be necessary in the course of the story to commit a forgery or a murder, it is not to be expected that the world will allow the crime to pass unpunished. But once the veracity and nobility, the magnanimity and self-sacrifice, which shall characterise this art and the professors of it, have raised the tone of the world, we shall be granted, I doubt not, the most cordial permission to execute atrocities, which, committed selfishly, would brand the criminal as an unnatural monster, but which, performed for art's sake, will redound everlastingly to the credit of the artist.'

Mrs. Lee looked helplessly at her brother, who whispered to her, 'Leave him to me. I'll make it all right.'

The two men then returned to the parlour, leaving Caroline to wait on Chartres.

Briscoe having cooled down, began to examine the possibilities of good and evil which might spring to himself from his dealing with Chartres. Entered on impulsively as little more than a practical joke; achieved so far with an apparent absolute success—a success which he now felt to be the most remarkable thing about it—this adventure, as he now viewed it, opened up a field for his enterprise which might produce wheat or tares according to his husbandry. He lit a pipe, stretched himself on the sofa, and, closing his eyes, concentrated his thoughts on the remarkable incident which he had brought about.

Lee, whose presence Briscoe had ignored, began to pace the room the moment his brother-in-law's eyes were shut. The stealthy, cat-like glance which he threw at Briscoe expanded to a blaze of triumph as, in one of his turns across the floor, he seized both portmanteaus, and, without accelerating his pace, walked into the unoccupied bedroom, the door of which he locked as softly as he could. Being relieved by Lee's withdrawal, Briscoe gave himself a shake on the sofa, and proceeded with his cogitation.

In the meantime Chartres had revived again. He was unable to use his tongue, but signed by opening his mouth that he wished to eat and drink. He nibbled a little toast and drank some water. He then surveyed the room and his nurse with close attention, and twice attempted to speak; but, failing to produce any other sound than a sigh, he turned his face to the wall and fell asleep.

Caroline went at once to the parlour, where, of course, she found her brother alone.

'Peter,' she said, 'what do you wish to do with this poor man?'

Briscoe uttered an exclamation of irritation and sat up to reply.

'What should we do with him?' he snarled crustily. 'Nothing, I suppose. Send him—— Where the devil are the portmanteaus?'

'And where's Maxwell?'

Briscoe was in the lobby immediately.

'Here's his hat!' he cried. 'He's not gone off.'

Before he had time to try the door of the room into which Lee had shut himself it opened, and that gentleman came forth. He was scented, gloved, and dressed in a black broadcloth suit, which had evidently never been worn before. He smiled to his brother-in-law, kissed his wife, and stepped jauntily into the parlour. They followed, amazed and silent.

'I am Henry Chartres,' he said, drawing a handful of bank-notes from a bulky purse and offering them to Caroline. Briscoe snatched them eagerly, and stowed them in his breast-pocket. At that moment the doorbell rang with a violent peal that paralysed the three. A visit at any moment was an unusual thing in their household; but Caroline, as she went to open the door, experienced a greater perturbation than she knew how to account for; and her feeling of dread was not lessened when the cabman, who had helped her brother to carry Chartres upstairs, and two policemen entered without ceremony. They walked past her into the parlour.

'Well, constable,' said Lee, addressing the foremost of the two officers, 'what's the matter?'

The constable turned to the cabman, and the cabman looked bewildered. When in the house before he had noticed the striking similarity between Lee and Chartres, and also the great apparent disparity between the social condition of his fare and that of the latter's professed relation. On returning to his stand, he communicated his doubts to the policemen who had been present at the accident. These two sapient Highlanders, after considerable discussion, concluded to call at the house to which the cabman had driven, and, if they found nothing suspicious, excuse their visit in any way suggested. The imaginations of the three had behaved in a felonious manner on the road. Peyton Street had certainly not the cleanest of reputations; and the cabman had got the length of arresting Briscoe's hand in the act of chopping up Chartres' left leg—being the last entire member of his body—when he met the man himself, as he supposed, smiling and as fresh as a daisy.

'We came to see how you were, sir,' said one of the policemen at last.

'Oh, I'm all right now,' said Lee, putting his hand in his pocket. 'I believe you assisted me when I fell. I'll see you downstairs,' with a nod which the constables understood as it was meant. 'I want you,' he said to the cabman, 'to drive me to St. Enoch Station. You'll get my portmanteaus here,' leading him to the bedroom in which he had changed his dress and name.

'Good-bye, Carry. Good-bye, Peter,' and before his wife and brother-in-law had recovered from their surprise, he was rattling away to the station.

CHAPTER II

THE SUITOR AND THE SUED

Miss Jane Chartres was a most emphatic talker, because she believed everything she said. Not that she always knew beforehand that what she might be going to say was true; but as soon as she found herself saying anything she believed it firmly from the moment of its announcement. If free-thinking people ever ventured to express a doubt that she might have been misinformed, she gave them her authorities. As the number of witnesses to Miss Jane's word was much too great to admit of their being named separately, she quoted them in the lump, and would silence at once the loudest infidel with a superemphatic, 'Everybody says so,' or 'Everybody does it.'

Miss Jane, being so well acquainted with the sayings and doings of everybody, had been forced to the belief, without knowing French, and with the inconsistency of genius, that everybody was a fool. She did not publish this dogma from the house-tops, but she did most sincerely believe it. About the time that she saw her way clearly to believe in the foolishness of everybody, another faith began to dawn upon her—a faith that she was the only individual in the world who was not a fool. It should hardly be called a faith either: for it never assumed the brightness and consistency of belief, but remained in an uncertain, nebulous condition, perhaps because she never really set herself to examine into the truth of the matter, allowing a sort of flickering halo of infallibility to play about the picture of herself which she beheld in her own mind.

Although she believed that it behoved everybody else, male and female, being fools, to marry, she had come to the conclusion that it behoved her, being in a measure a wise woman, to remain single. This opinion, like all her other opinions—her constant opinions, that is—had been of gradual growth. It was generally supposed that it had fairly taken root about her thirtieth year, when a certain lawyer, who had been a great friend presumably of her brother, discontinued his visits to Snell House, and took to wife the wealthy widow of a game-dealer. It was understood that time had made four prior attempts with the help of a mill-owner, a wealthy farmer, a minister, and a retired colonel, to dibble this opinion with regard to herself and marriage into the soil of Miss Jane's mind. On the marriage of the lawyer with the game-dealer's widow, time made a furious stab with his persevering instrument, and the hardy opinion took a strong hold, and grew, and flourished, and put forth a flower. The opinion was that she ought not to marry; the flower, that she was made for a higher end than to be the wife of any man. The fragrance of this flower was grateful to her. However, she never forgot that it was only the blossom of an opinion, liable to be uprooted, and not the sculptured ornament of an impossible-to-be-disestablished faith.

At the time when our story begins—the middle of July, 1880—Miss Jane had been absolute mistress of Snell House for three months, her brother William, a bachelor, with whom she had lived for a number of years, having died suddenly in the spring. A stroke of apoplexy had overtaken him while walking alone, as his habit was, on the shore road. His brother, Henry Chartres, was in India at the time, having gone out when a young man to push his fortune. Within five years he had secured by his own energy, and with some monetary help from his brother, a partnership in a lucrative business. He then married a lady of some means, who brought him only one child, a daughter, called Muriel, after her mother. As is the custom, the girl was brought to the home-country to be educated, her father taking a six months' holiday for the purpose of seeing her safely installed in his brother's house, where she was to remain for some time, in order to become acclimatised, before going to her first boarding-school, and also that she might not feel so sorely her separation from her father and mother, as she would have done had she gone at once among strangers. Shortly after the return of Henry Chartres to India his wife died. He at once determined to give up business and return to Scotland, where the society of his daughter and relatives would console him for the loss of his wife. But a crisis in the affairs of the Calcutta house of which he was a principal kept him in India. His foresight and resource were absolutely necessary for the weathering of the storm; and he found the relief, which he had been about to seek in Scotland, in an unreserved devotion to business. When he had re-established the credit of his firm more securely than ever, it became apparent that, were he to retire, the consequences might be disastrous for his partners, as his name had come to be synonymous with stability. It was, therefore, not until ten years after the death of his wife that he felt himself at liberty to give up business. The news of his brother's death arrived just as he had begun to arrange his affairs. In reply to a telegram from his sister, he bade her expect him in July; and announced in his first letter that he would manage to reach Scotland about the middle of the month.

The lands of Snell consist of a bit of moor and a park. They had been bought in the beginning of last century by the first notable member of the west country Chartreses, a branch of an old Perthshire family. Miss Jane Chartres refused altogether to admit that she knew anything of the derivation of her ancestor's wealth; and we, therefore, think it needless to refer further to the subject. The wall which bounded Snell Park on the north stood about fifty yards from the edge of a moderately high cliff overlooking the Firth of Clyde. The top of this wall was four feet from the ground within the park, and a little over six feet above the road without. The road was private, and scarcely better than a foot-path.

For three months, then, Miss Jane Chartres, whose character has been indicated above, whose age is left to the reader's charity, had exercised despotic power over Snell House, moor, park, and north wall. But liberties had been taken with that wall, and with an old tree that grew against it. The reader shall hear the history of these dreadful doings from Miss Jane's own lips. She was there, beside the tree, on the afternoon of July 15; and, with her, her friend Mr. Alec Dempster, a very wealthy youth of thirty, with no past—the brother of Emily Dempster, Miss Jane's one bosom friend, whose place in her affections, vacant by death, he supplied in a sort of interim capacity as well as a man with no past, and no possibility of ever having one, could be expected to do.

'Well, Mr. Dempster,' said Miss Jane, 'aren't you dying with wonder to know why I've brought you here?'

'Dying?' said Mr. Dempster, whose voice was a reminiscence of some mechanical sound, one couldn't exactly say which; 'dying is such a strong expression that it almost—eh—ah—expresses the degree of my wonder.'

Mr. Dempster moved his head spirally, slowly and regularly from the top to the bottom of something, as he spoke. That was the great peculiarity of Mr. Dempster: he was like something. Everything about him, from his boots to his manners, bore indefinable resemblances to other things; but the moment a simile seemed securely anchored in some characteristic of his appearance or conduct the characteristic would undulate into something so incongruous with the simile that the latter was like a pair of spectacles on a lynx. One thing only he insisted on reproducing with some degree of regularity of form: the spiral wriggle of his head—extending occasionally into his body—which always accompanied the effort to speak, and sometimes occurred alone.

'Read that,' said Miss Jane, handing Mr. Dempster a letter.

Mr. Dempster, mildly astonished and looking like something very foolish, did as he was directed.

'MY DARLING FRANK,—Meet me to-morrow at five, at the low wall. It's half-past ten, and I am very sleepy. I've been reading history to aunt since eight. I am beginning to dream already, before I am asleep. It's a happy dream—about you! It will become bright and plain when I get to sleep. Good-night, sweetheart.—Your own MURIEL.'

'What do you think of that?' snapped Miss Jane; and Mr. Dempster looked in all directions hurriedly, as if a whip had been cracked about his ears.

'It's—it's very frank,' he said.

'Very,' went on Miss Jane. 'Look at that.'

She pointed to the bole of the huge elm beneath whose boughs they were standing, indicating a little space denuded of the ivy which covered the rest of the trunk, and extended along the four great arms, and up among the smaller branches of the tree.

Mr. Dempster bored his nose into the uncovered bark, studied it from several points of view, bending and curvetting and bridling with as much ado as if he had been an antiquary in presence of a newly-discovered inscription.

'"M C, F H,"' he said at length; 'inside a heart—very pretty and—ah—suggestive; but—commonplace.'

Mr. Dempster's pauses, however arbitrary, were impressive.

'Do you know whose these initials are?' Miss Jane asked.

'I haven't the remotest idea.'

'"M C," Muriel Chartres; "F H," Frank Hay.'

'Ah!'

Dempster leant against an arm of the tree and regarded Miss Jane blankly. He had arrived from Edinburgh that day at her summons, to meet Mr. Chartres, who was expected in the afternoon, and to prosecute his suit for the hand of Muriel. This was a dash of cold water right in his face. He hadn't a word to say, and scarcely any breath to say one.

'You know Mr. Hay,' Miss Jane said. 'You remember, William used to patronise him.'

'The foundling! Why, the fellow hasn't a penny!' exclaimed Dempster.

'Ah, Mr. Dempster,' said Miss Jane more sweetly than her wont, 'presumption is poverty's next door neighbour, wealth and modesty often go hand in hand.'

Dempster at once applied this aphoristic compliment to himself, as he was intended to do; but he horrified Miss Jane by bowing emphatically in acknowledgment, and he outraged her further by endeavouring to pay her back in kind:

'A thorough acquaintance with the world generally accompanies the single life.'

That was his period, and he imagined he had acquitted himself fairly well. But dissatisfaction lowered in Miss Jane's brow. He proceeded with stammering haste to mend matters:

'Especially the single female—eh—ah——'

An angry flush drew him up. Still, he went at it again headlong, smiling too, and in as suave a tone as he could command:

'Wisdom is an old maid—I mean—Minerva was unmarried.'

Everybody knows people like Mr. Dempster. We are accustomed to their shifting similitudes, their inability to express themselves, their pretensions, and their good nature. In fact, we do not regard them—we do not recognise that they are peculiar; and when we see one of them singled out and reproduced—on the stage, for example—however faithfully, we call it caricature. Miss Jane had a very narrow circle of acquaintances. The Chartreses, indeed, were all proud originals. For several generations they had mingled little in society, preferring to retain their angularities of character in all the ruggedness of nature, rather than submit to the painful process of grinding on the social wheel, by which jagged, dull-veined flints are smoothed and polished. Miss Jane could not tolerate ordinary people. Dempster was the only commonplace character in whom she had any interest. His visits to Snell House had been hitherto few and short, and she had never got accustomed to his genial stupidity. Ineptitude with Miss Jane was an almost unpardonable offence. She remembered, however, in the confusion to which he had reduced her, much necessity in the past for self-denial and longsuffering on his account, and, having a real regard for him, she calmed her troubled soul, saying to herself, 'He means well.' And then aloud:

'Now, Mr. Dempster, this is the low wall Muriel speaks of. This letter I found here.'

She pushed aside some large ivy leaves in one of the forks of the elm, and deposited the letter in a deep, natural crevice—the bottom of which was quite invisible, although easily reached by the hand.

'How did you know to search there?' asked Dempster.

'Because I knew Muriel was in love.'

'Did she tell you?'

'No, no; this was the way of it.'

Miss Jane was in her element. She leant against the bole of the tree and folded her arms across her belt.

'I observed that she had acquired a habit of going about with her eyebrows absurdly elevated, with a languishing look in her eyes, and with her lips just touching each other; but evidently ready at a moment's notice to open and sigh, or to compress and kiss. I knew very well what these signs meant in a girl of her age. Just raise your eyebrows, Mr. Dempster.'

Mr. Dempster raised his eyebrows.

'No, no! not to the extent of expressing astonishment, but in this way. See.'

Miss Jane suited the action to the word.

'When you raise your eyebrows that way your eyes can't help a languishing expression. Then this is the way her mouth was.'

Miss Jane made a *moue*.

'If you don't care to do it before me, do it when you are alone, and you will find that raising your eyebrows and looking at nothing, and preparing the lips to open, will produce in you a relaxed, sentimental, self-pitying kind of feeling, which is pretty like what romantic girls feel when they are in love. Of course, in Muriel's case it was the feeling which produced the expression, and not the expression the feeling; but I know very well that an assumption of the expression can produce the feeling, and that it always conveys the idea of that feeling to those who see it. It's the same with all feelings.'

The whole man Dempster had listened to this exposition, and burst out earnestly, 'Miss Chartres, your experience amazes me! Your observation is that of a keen—eh—ah—observer; and your discernment is truly marvellous!'

He always tried to talk in newspaper paragraphs, but his efforts were seldom attended with the success they merited.

Miss Jane shrugged her shoulders and continued: 'My suspicions were confirmed yesterday. I followed her here and secured this letter. I thought it right that you, as a suitor for Muriel's hand, favoured by me, and doubtless to be favoured by her father, should be informed of the matter.'

'You overpower me with kindness,' blurted Dempster. 'And you'll stand by me, Miss Chartres? You'll be my go-between—I mean my bulwark, my bottle-holder?' He was full of imagery, but he qualified it, saying plaintively: 'I can't express myself lucidly and vividly, like you; but everybody knows I mean well.'

'I think we understand each other, Mr. Dempster,' said Miss Jane, looking at her watch. 'A quarter to five. We'd better go. Muriel will be here immediately. Of course I haven't told her that I have discovered this clandestine correspondence. I shall put the matter into her father's hands this very day, and leave him to deal with her.'

Dempster assented to this as a wise proceeding. 'It would hardly do to watch the meeting here, I suppose—that is, if there is a meeting,' he said, as they left the wall.

'To play the spy, Mr. Dempster! No, not that.'

The ivy-clad elm in which Miss Jane had found Muriel's letter, and in which she now left it forgetfully, was believed by the school-boys to mark the burial-place of a Roman general. It certainly looked as if it might be fourteen hundred years old, or even as old as the Christian era. It was a worthy peer of the Mongewell, Chipstead, and Spratborough elms, by the hoary roughness of its bark, where that could be seen, by its portly waist, and wide-spread arms, drooping gracefully to the ground, by its magnificent cone of foliage, and its fathomless depth of green. How pleasant Muriel found it to stand under, to lean against, to delight her eyes with its shapeliness, and bathe her sight in its ocean of colour! And then, with all its old-world dignity, how tender it was! How safe in its arms she felt! She could think and dream there like Nature herself, conscious and glad that the elm knew all about it. When she forced her way among the drooping boughs up to the mighty bole, she was sure that the tree thrilled with happiness, and she heard it murmuring—murmuring under its spicy breath. No wonder she made it her trysting-tree!

As soon as Miss Jane and Dempster returned to the house, Muriel, who had been lying on the lawn pretending to read a newspaper, arose, and, still apparently engrossed by the news, took a circuitous route to the elm. When she got beyond the range of prying eyes, the deceptive newspaper was folded, and, carrying it in one hand behind her, and in the other swinging by the strings her garden-hat, she sped along, fearful lest Frank should have to wait. Half over the wall she stretched herself, and looked up and down the road. She was first. She leant against the tree and gazed before her. She felt perfectly happy. He was sure to come; and that was the horizon—the end of the world. There was nothing beyond the little quarter of an hour that was dawning like a new era. She would hardly be so happy when he, the sun of it, came to kiss her.

Now she looked out through the screen of leaves, softening the light upon their scabrous cheeks, and showering it like dew from their downy breasts, and saw, latticed by the wiry, corky branches and bright brown callow twigs, the violet Firth, smooth, velvety, the pasture of white gulls, whose cries come faintly up; glimpses of the opposite shore, with the sparkling houses of the summer towns; the lordly sweep of the entrance to Loch Long; the purple misty crowns of the Cobbler and Ben Donich; and the sky; and a shadow—

'Frank!'

'How glad I am to find you here!' he said. 'I was foolish enough to fear you mightn't come.'

'Why did you doubt? I never missed meeting you yet.'

'Then you expected me! I was sure at the bottom of my heart that you would be here.'

'Did I expect you! What are you thinking of? There's something the matter. How could you possibly be afraid that I mightn't come after I had asked you to meet me?'

'But you didn't ask me.'

'Oh! Did you not get my message?'

'No; and I visited our letter-box last night and this morning.'

She tore her arm from his, and plunged her hand into the fork of the tree. A shock passed through her as she felt her letter. She knew in a moment it had been violated. The thought that another than he for whom it was intended had read it thrilled her with an exquisite pang. Her whole face and neck flushed crimson. She drew out the paper, crushed it small, and thrust it into her pocket.

'The mean, shameful spy!' she hissed.

Youth has no mercy in a case of this kind.

'See,' she continued, panting, 'I put it here this morning at eight. It was gone at ten. Now it is here again. The traitor!'

'Is it a man?' asked Frank.

'No! It's——'

She had grown pale, and she blushed again. She looked at him with flickering eyelids. The foolish fellow's pride in Muriel at that moment made him heartsick; the lump was in his throat, and, had he been unobserved, the moisture which stood in his eyes would have overflowed. Even in the first wild anger at betrayal she would not betray again. He placed his arm about her and she sobbed; one sob, and then one tear out of each eye; and with that she mastered herself.

'Frank,' she said, as if the discovery had not been made, 'you know my father will be here to-day. He may have come while I've been talking to you. Will you speak to him to-night? I don't want to have a secret from him. Will you? You needn't be frightened. I haven't seen him since I was nine; but I know that he's like you, gentle and manly—just a gentleman. Make up your mind now—quick, quick, quick! And let me away, or I'll be late for dinner.'

And so it was arranged that they should see each other at the low-walk again at eight that evening, lest there should be any reason why Frank might not speak at once to Mr. Chartres.

CHAPTER III

ON THE ROAD

Lee secured a compartment for himself in the Greenock train. He had a large bundle of letters, taken from one of Chartres' portmanteaus, with him. These he studied with an intensity which he had never bestowed on anything before. He selected some dozen for perusal, and was still devouring them when the train arrived at Princes Pier.

As he stepped on the platform he reeled and was only saved from falling by the porter who opened the door of the compartment in which he had travelled. This weakness was the result of the strain of the last two hours. He fortified himself with a glass of brandy and a sandwich, deposited the portmanteaus in the left-luggage office; and started to walk to Gourock.

He was a tall man, with more than proportionate length of limb. Walking had always been his favourite exercise, and he looked along the Greenock esplanade from the summit of the approach to the station with a shining eye. All the world has admired it from the deck of the *Columba*; but to walk along it at a good spanking pace, feeling its costly breadth, its substantiality, its triumph over nature; to be conscious of the solid nineteenth-century comfort and luxury that line one side of it, ascending the hill to larger villas and more spacious grounds; and to be, as Lee became, before he was two minutes on the road, part and parcel of the sky-blue lake-like firth, whose water murmured, for the tide was full, with soft reproach against the curbing bastion; of the shining magical houses on the other side; of the green and golden shoreward slopes; of the depths and heights of the purple mountains that met the sky—to be drunk with the sunlight and the sea, with the merging, glowing, fading wealth of colour, and the far-reaching romance of the hills, is to enjoy to the full this west-country esplanade.

When he arrived at the end of it, Lee, unable to endure the ordinary road, jumped on a car and took a seat on the top.

He was now in a mood to dare anything, and continued his revel in the splendid July afternoon, for the brain-sick man was a poet.

Through Gourock and Ashton the car rattled, but, wrapped in his own dream, he saw nothing of them.

From the terminus he walked confidently along the shore road. He felt that he would know Snell House the moment he beheld it. Then there would be no difficulty. Chartres could not be expected to remember any of the domestics; besides, in ten years it was more than likely that they had all been changed twice over. His sister and daughter—he could not possibly mistake them. He would be shy a little, undemonstrative, uncommunicative, and plead his long journey—for Chartres had travelled from London on the preceding night—as an excuse for retiring early. Then——

A sudden slap on the shoulder interrupted his reverie, and, wheeling round, he confronted Briscoe, on whose face a bitter sneer was varnished over with a grin at the surprise and annoyance his appearance caused his brother-in-law.

'This way,' said Briscoe; and Lee followed him in silence.

They found a seat, one of a number placed along the shore between the Cloch and Ashton. There was a considerable slope from the road to the water's edge; and they were securely concealed from the eyes of pedestrians by the trees and bushes that line stretches of the sea-board.

It never entered Lee's head to ask Briscoe how he came to be there. Had he done so, Briscoe would have told him—that is, if he had thought the truth expedient—how Caroline and he, after Lee's sudden and daring departure from Peyton Street, judged it the best course to intercept him at the St. Enoch station; but how he, Briscoe, having already in his breast-pocket some of the advantages arising from Lee's deception, determined, if possible, to add to them, and so journeyed to Greenock in the same train with his brother-in-law; and, pushing on before him, waited for him at a quiet part of the road, where they might discuss the situation without much fear of interruption or observation. He had not the remotest intention of aiding Lee, whom he despised, to pursue his deception to a successful issue. On the contrary, he intended to line his own pockets as thickly as he could, and get off to London that night or the following morning. There was one risk: Chartres might recover sufficiently to come down to Snell House before he had gone. This risk he determined to run.

'I wish,' said Lee, recovering speedily from his surprise, 'you had not come down yet. I have been thinking of you and Caroline, and don't exactly see what to do with you.'

His infatuation was such that he had no doubt Briscoe intended to collaborate with him.

'I might marry you,' he continued, 'to my daughter Muriel; or, as she is perhaps too young, to my mature sister, Jane. But what to do with Caroline? You see, I didn't marry again in India. The only course I can conceive at present, will be to make her acquaintance as it were for the first time, and marry her over again. But there's no hurry; and, I think, on the whole, you had better return to Glasgow until I prepare matters for you down here.'

'Mr. Chartres,' said Briscoe, 'am I to collaborate with you, or am I not?'

Lee flushed with pleasure, and answered, 'Most certainly, my dear Peter!'

'Then I must have some share in devising the plot.'

'Assuredly! I beg your pardon. I was forgetting your rights. Really, I have been selfish in the solitary enjoyment of the creation of this novel, which you began with such originality and power.'

Briscoe rather winced at this. However, he was glad to find Lee so tractable.

'Mr. Chartres,' he said, 'I am your friend, Mr. Peter Briscoe. I came from India with you. I'm a rough diamond; don't care how I dress—accounts for my rather worn toggery; see? Saved you from drowning when you fell overboard in the Bay of Biscay. You, eternally grateful; I, no friends in this country—across for a visit merely—came right north with you, agreeing to do so at the last moment, so that you had no time to advise them at Snell House.'

Lee gazed at his brother-in-law with admiration.

'Briscoe, my dear fellow,' he cried, 'you're a trump! You—you saved my life.'

'Then we'll take the road again,' said Briscoe. 'The house is round the corner; I inquired shortly before you came up.'

'Briscoe,' said Lee, 'for the first work of a newlyborn art, we are——'

'Beating the record.'

'Exactly, my rough and ready friend.'

CHAPTER IV

A HEAVY FATHER

'Now, Jane, let me understand this about Muriel. You say she is at present engaged in a grand love affair with some young hopeful or other.'

'Yes, Henry. Frank Hay is a very good-looking, clever, well-behaved young man. He has taken one of the big bursaries in Glasgow University, and looks forward to a professorship somewhere. These prospects are rather mediocre, especially in connection with a Chartres; but neither William nor I would have said a word against him were he not a foundling.'

'A foundling! How very interesting! An actual foundling.'

'O, there's nothing unusual about his case. I forget the exact details, but they differ in no essential from what we are accustomed to in stories.'

'That's rather unfortunate. I should have liked everything connected with these events to have the same characteristic as the main circumstance, distinct novelty.'

'What do you mean, Henry? Muriel is right in thinking you curiously changed.'

'Does she think so? Well; I should have stuck by my original determination, and gone to bed; but I felt so invigorated after dinner, that I thought we might as well have a talk over matters this evening.'

'Yes,' said Miss Jane, dryly, prodding Lee all over with her piercing eyes.

'Do you think,' she queried, 'we did right in forbidding Muriel to have any communication with Mr. Hay?'

'Well, my dear sister, you must see that the question of right hardly enters here. It is purely a matter of adapting means to an end. Should the course you have followed, as in the case of a pair of high-spirited lovers, be calculated to lead to strained relations, and produce, say, an elopement, I should be inclined to support you; as, although shorn of much of its romance in these days of railways and telegraphs, there is always a measure of excitement to be got out of a runaway match.'

Miss Jane meditated for several seconds; and hopefully came to the conclusion that her brother had developed a satirical tendency, which he gratified in this recondite fashion. She made no reply. Lee resumed.

'I think you had better send Muriel to me. I would like to have a talk with her alone.'

'Very well,' said Miss Jane curtly, and left the room.

It was the library in which Lee sat. He had arrived with Briscoe about six o'clock, just as the Snell household were sitting down to dinner. Four was the usual dinner hour, but it had been put off till five and then till six—to the anger and horror of the cook—in the hope that Mr. Chartres would be there to preside. Both Lee and Briscoe imagined that the dinner had gone off to admiration. The latter, taking advantage of his rollicking character, was now roving about the rooms, helping himself to many little valuables. After securing all the money Lee was possessed of, which he might manage to do that evening, he saw a fair chance of getting away with his booty, out of immediate danger, and before the arrival of Chartres, whom he half-expected to find in every room he entered. He knew that Caroline would not wait for his return if her charge recovered sufficiently to travel, but would start with him at once; and while she might be able to make terms for her crazy husband, some stout menservants and a duck-pond suggested anything but a pleasant ending to his own share in the adventure. After Miss Jane had left the library, Lee, with a most placid expression, walked across the room once or twice, and sat down to wait for Muriel. In a second or two the door opened, and Mr. Dempster appeared. This gentleman had been left to himself since dinner, and was searching for Miss Jane.

'I beg your pardon, sir,' he said, looking the very picture of a square man in a round hole. 'I thought Miss Chartres was here.'

'Come in, come in, Mr. Dempster,' said Lee, blandly. 'Is it my daughter or my sister you wish to see?'

'Your sister, sir.'

'I expect them both here in a few minutes. Take a seat.'

Dempster gathered his coat-tails on either side with as much tenderness and delicacy as if they had been growing out of him and were recovering from rheumatism, and sat down on the very edge of a chair, crowding himself together as if he had consisted of several people.

'I hope I don't intrude,' said Dempster, with the spiral motion of his head. He was always more uncomfortable and serpentine than usual in the presence of strangers.

'Not at all.'

Lee said to himself, 'This is a millionaire; and I am an adventurer—Fortune is a mistress of irony.'

A smile peculiar to him, and childish in its unconcealed expression of pleasure, passed over his face. Then he said brusquely, but with perfect good humour, 'Do you think much, Mr. Dempster?'

'Think!' exclaimed Mr. Dempster, throwing his head back in a convolution which a burlesque actor would have paid highly to learn the trick of.

'Yes, think,' repeated Lee, with his happy, innocent smile.

'I—I can't say I do,' said Dempster, perspiring profusely. 'I—I,' he continued making a wholly ineffectual effort to laugh—'I—eh—ah—haven't given the subject much attention. But——'

'Exactly, Mr. Dempster, I understand. I have often thought by the way, that you unlucky fellows who inherit your money, can't enjoy it so well as we who have wrought for it.'

Now, if there was one thing Dempster objected to more than another, it was to be hurried about from subject to subject. He had just got his mind focussed to the consideration of Lee's first question, when a new distance intervened, and—he saw men as trees walking. But he must make some reply.

'No—no,' he said. 'We can't. I—I think we can't. Eh—ah——'

'Eh—ah,' the favourite expletive of the orator, was frequently employed by Dempster with a solemn pathos inexpressibly touching. Lee almost relented at the overpowering sadness of its utterance on this occasion: but the baiting of a millionaire was as novel as any of his present manifold pleasures, and he continued it.

'I suppose now,' he said, 'you would like to work hard at something or other. Most idle men would.'

Dempster rubbed his knees with vehemence, anxious, doubtless, to get himself into an electric condition which would enable him to overcome the insane disposition he felt to fall forward at Lee's feet. He succeeded in producing so much of the positive fluid as to fall back instead of forward; but all he could manage to say was, 'I suppose I would.'

'I have often wondered,' said Lee, whose smile was beginning to be warped by malice, 'why rich men don't commit burglaries and homicides in order to obtain terms of hard labour. It would be such an absolute change for them; *ennui* would hide its head.'

It is impossible to say what ultimate effect this remarkable suggestion would have had upon Dempster, for the paralysis which it caused to begin with was suddenly cured by a tap—a shrinking, single tap on the door, preceding the entrance of Muriel. Dempster took the opportunity of escaping in a thoroughly graceless manner. When the door had closed again, Lee said to Muriel, who remained standing, 'Do you not find me exactly what you expected?'

She looked hard at him. It was on her lips to tell him that she thought him very unlike his letters; but she merely said, 'You are not like your photographs.'

'No; they were generally thought good in India.'

'O, anyone could tell for whom they were meant.'

'Of course. My appearance has changed since I last sat to a photographer. Sit down, Muriel; I wish to have some serious conversation with you.'

Muriel sat down on a couch. Her eyes were twinkling, and the blood danced into her cheeks.

'I have learned from your aunt,' said Lee, who was just a little too portentously grave, 'that there exists a romantic attachment between a certain Mr. Frank Hay and you. I understand you are firmly persuaded that you and this gentleman love each other with an unchangeable love. I will grant that Mr. Hay is a handsome, high-spirited young man. I do not remember to have seen him; but I give my daughter credit for not falling in love with a booby. I admit that first love is the most ecstatically delightful thing in the world. I say, I subscribe to all that and as much more as you like in the same strain; but—' and here he became very severe—'I have to inform you that from this day you must cease to see, or correspond with Mr. Frank Hay.'

'O father!'

Lee, enjoying his power, and as much a spectator of the scene as an actor in it, continued coldly, 'It will be hard I know; but your friends have acted very wisely in coming between you. Girls should never be allowed to choose husbands, and never are in well-regulated families. You may think me plain-spoken and harsh, perhaps; but I have a habit of coming to the point; and, notice, of never returning to it. The matter is settled.'

'But, sir——'

'What! have I not said it is settled? I do not mean, however, to do you out of a husband.'

Muriel shivered, and her face became white.

'My friend, Mr. Briscoe, who saved my life is still a young man; and I intend to have him for a son-in-law.'

Lee's eyes dilated with exultation. His novel was going to turn out a masterpiece.

'Marry Mr. Briscoe!'

'It rests with him,' said Lee.

'What! Your daughter must marry this Mr. Briscoe if he wants her, whether she likes or not?'

'I am glad,' said Lee in a truly regal style, 'that you apprehend the matter so clearly.'

'I am bewildered,' said Muriel.

'You seem to be; but it is wise of you not to object. I hope to find you always a dutiful daughter.'

Lee left the room. A time-piece on the mantelshelf rang eight. The blood returned to Muriel's cheeks, and she ran out of the house to the north wall.

CHAPTER V

THE ART OF PROPOSING

When Dempster left the library on the entrance of Muriel, he met Miss Jane at the door of that room. She proposed a turn in the park as the evening was doing honour to the glorious day. They went out together and wandered to Muriel's elm. Dempster's suit was the subject they discussed. She urged him to make a proposal that night, and promised to procure him an opportunity. Dempster was willing, but in great straits how to proceed.

'You see,' he said, 'I never did a thing of the kind before. Then you know Muriel is not aware that I'm in love with her. If she knew that, then I could go at it like a—professor.'

It is to be feared he intended to say 'nigger,' and only substituted the more refined but equally enigmatic word by an exhaustive effort of brain power, whose external manifestation was the usual wriggle.

Miss Jane said, 'Well it *is* very difficult to know what to do in making an offer of marriage. I have had six proposals—that is, formal proposals—all of which I refused peremptorily, as I think that I was made for a higher end than to be the wife of any man—and they were all done differently; but, on the whole, I prefer the colonel's method; and I think in proposing to Muriel you had better follow it.'

'Oh, thank you! Tell me exactly what he did, and I'll practise it just now.'

In his excitement Dempster's body, lithe and lissom as that of the most poetical maiden, partook in the motion of his head. Miss Jane, who had often been on the point of speaking to him about this absurd habit, burst out, 'Don't wriggle that way, as if you were impaled!'

Dempster shrivelled up, and hung flaccid on his spinal column, like a hooked worm that has been long in the water.

'I assure you,' continued Miss Jane, less harshly, 'if you are ever to take a place in the world you must overcome that.'

'Must I! I'm very glad you've told me. It's my natural form.'

'Conquer it, conquer it. Remember Demosthenes, Mr. Dempster.'

'I will, I will,' he cried, almost breaking his back, and causing a hot shooting pain in his head, as he nipped a sprouting corkscrew in the bud—a metaphor worthy of himself. Then he made a sudden plunge into a sea of words, where he had to keep perpetually rapping on the head an electric eel that tried with unremitting fervour to run, or rather wriggle, the gauntlet of his body and escape by his skull through the suture.

'Miss Chartres,' he said, 'I wish you would help me. I have been wanting to get married for six years now, and I can't. I won't be caught. They try it, the mothers. They dangle their daughters before me like—like Mayflies. But I won't bite. I'd sooner starve, Miss Chartres, starve. Die in a ditch—celibacy, you know. I'll never marry one of these artificial flies. They may be good enough; but it's their mothers—O, their mothers! Why, I've read about them in novels. And then, when I do fall in love with a nice—with a sweet—a natural—eh—ah—a natural fly—you understand—I—I can't bite—haven't the courage—don't know how. I've been in love before several times—though I never loved anybody before like Muriel—and I couldn't possibly manage to—to bite. But you'll teach me now, my dear Miss Chartres.'

He emerged, dripping, and the long-repressed eel shot out at the crown of his head in a rapid spasm, leaving him a mere husk propped against the elm.

Miss Jane, who had made up her mind that he should marry Muriel, put his sincerity against his *gaucherie*, and determined to drill him into some better form; for she judged that if the excitement of talking about a proposal produced effects of the kind she had witnessed, that of making one would simply stultify its object.

'I'll help you,' she said. 'Stand there.'

She seated herself on a protruding root of the elm, and pointed to a sort of alcove in one of the large boughs. Dempster squeezed himself under the branches, and stood, or rather stooped, at attention.

'Now, obey my instructions. Imagine this to be a drawing-room. Come forward on tip-toe, and say very significantly, and in fact intensely, "Good evening. Miss Chartres," and don't wriggle.'

Dempster, clothed with resolution as with a strait-jacket, advanced, and whispered between his set teeth, 'Good evening, Miss Chartres.'

'Good evening, Mr. Dempster; be seated.'

He looked about for as comfortable a knot as possible, but Miss Jane cried, 'No, no! you must refuse respectfully. The gallant colonel did. He said something like this:—"Miss Chartres, I will never sit in your presence until I have got an answer to a question which my whole being is burning to ask." When you have said that, go down on one knee and take my hand.'

Dempster was beginning to feel at home. Miss Jane was so sympathetic, and smiled so benignly. In the heat of the moment, and to prove himself an apt scholar, he thought he would reproduce his lesson with variations. So he got down on his knees at the off-set, and began, 'My adored Miss Chartres, never again in your enchanting presence——'

'O!' went off among the branches like a sharp tap on a muffled drum.

Miss Jane looked up in time to catch a glimpse of Muriel's head. Dempster's strait-jacket snapped, and the released mechanism hoisted him to his feet, spinning and glaring round in a vortex of coat-tails.

Miss Jane, also on her feet, said calmly, 'That was Muriel. There's no harm done. I must just tell her the exact state of the case. It's always best to tell the truth. If she has any heart at all it will be touched at the thought of your rehearsing your proposal. I'll go after her, and explain, and send her to you. That's the very thing.'

Now Miss Jane was a very shrewd woman. Her mind had been ingenuously fixed on a marriage between her niece and her *protege*, up to the moment of the appearance of Muriel's head among the branches. There and then a sense of the incongruity of such a union had struck her with most convincing power. Several forces converged in this blow. One can be mentioned unreservedly, viz., the sudden intuitive recognition of the fact that Muriel would never consent to marry Dempster. Another, equally powerful, must only be hinted:—the lady at that moment had once more, however strangely, a gentleman at her feet. These are the keys to her future conduct.

She was about to go after Muriel, but Dempster clutched her dress.

'I can't,' he whimpered.

'Nonsense. You'll be astonished at your own courage.'

'But the proposal. How am I to say it?'

'Keep a good heart, and remember my instructions. I've told you how to begin. The rest you must do for yourself. Muriel will he here shortly.'

Dempster resigned himself: and in a few seconds fear wound him up to a pitch of nervous excitement, abnormal even with him.

'I'll rehearse again,' he said aloud, withdrawing to the alcove. He got into the strait-jacket once more, and advanced on tip-toe to an imaginary lady. But the charge did not give him satisfaction. He retreated and stepped out a second time. He was too absorbed in his manoeuvres to remember that however perfect he might become, this mode would be out of the question in the impending interview.

'Good evening,' he said impressively to the mossy root, and got down on his knees.

'Miss Chartres'—and persuasion tipped his tongue—'I am burning to know——'

A silvery ripple glided through the air behind him. 'I beg' pardon, Mr. Dempster. I was not aware you were so pious a man,' said Muriel.

A jack-in-the-box when the spring is touched shoots up not more suddenly than Dempster did. Abashed, he could only stammer, 'Eh—ah—I mean well.'

'I do indeed believe you,' said Muriel in a kindly tone. 'My aunt has told me that you were about to honour me with an offer of marriage. I thank you, sir; but I beg you not to put me to the necessity—the very disagreeable necessity—of refusing you.'

Half-an-hour before she could not have taken such a plain-spoken initiative; but the interview with Lee had roused her soul to arms.

Dempster, on the contrary, dimly conscious of his own absurdity and afraid to trust his nature, stood forth against her in his strait-waistcoat of formality. He could hardly believe his ears, accustomed to the lie that no girl could possibly refuse a millionaire, a false tenet which he had donned with his first pair of trousers.

'Why should you refuse me? I—I am very rich, and I love you.' This was still pronounced in his best society tone.

'I am very sorry for you,' said Muriel frigidly. 'If you persist you will only annoy us both.'

His fear suddenly left him. He felt an underhand attack upon his wealth, which was *him*—his personality. He threw off the strait-waistcoat. He turned up the sleeves of his riches, and, in a raucous tone like that of an aggrieved school bully who wants an excuse to pommel a small boy, said 'Why do you refuse me? Give me a reason.'

'A reason!'

'Yes. Is there anything extraordinary in asking for a reason? I can't be put off in this way, you know. Do you love another?'

'I am very sorry for you; but you are becoming impertinent.'

'But what am I to do if you won't marry me? All my friends know what I've come here for. It's absurd.'

'You had better desist.'

It is charitable to suppose that Dempster was utterly unaware of what he was doing. Anger nearly suffocated him. He twisted and squirmed at every word, writhing with the anticipation of mockery.

'It's shameful,' he cried. 'Here have I been loving you like—like lava; and to be thrown overboard, ignominiously—yes, ignominiously'—he fancied he heard the word resounding in smoking-rooms—'for a poor nobody.'

Muriel started and glared at him. But he was 'fey,' and went on.

'You may well look! A foundling—a charity-boy! You love this sup—superfluous and probably illegitimate pauper, who———'

'O, you unmanly fool!'

'I say!' and he fell against the tree smitten by Muriel's thunder and lightning. The storm pealed on.

'I have read of men who spoke such cowardice, but I never thought to know one. How dare you talk of love? O the shame! Every wealthy fool can look at us, and love us, as they say, and whine to us—it *is* a shame! What right have you to love me or think of me? If you ever wish to be worth a thought, or fit for his service whom you've slandered, go and found hospitals, endow scholarships—fling your wealth in the sea—only get rid of it! And plough the fields, break stones, dig ditches—some honest work your scanty brains are suited for; and when that has made you something of a man, go and beg his pardon. Go away from here, now, at once. He's waiting for me.'

Dempster limped away. His works were all run down. Youth is cruel, and Muriel had meant to wound; but she felt a little remorseful at the sight of the abject creature she had scorched and scotched with such crude severity, and wished that she had at least spared him the last savage cut. To be called a fool and a coward—to be told to get rid of one's personality, is bad; but to be dismissed in order to make instant room for the other, partakes too much of hacking and slashing, and might even be put in the category with vitriol-throwing.

Muriel looked over the wall and called Frank. He was waiting somewhere near, she knew; and he came and climbed over and kissed her.

'Where were you hiding?' she asked.

'I sat on a stone by the side of the wall, and meant to sit there till the voices ceased, or you called me.'

'Did you hear what we said?'

'No.'

'Well, it doesn't matter just now. I'll tell you some other time.'

She sat down on the wall and bade him do the same. Dempster was forgotten: the stronger impression, that produced by Lee, came out through the more recent one like the original writing on a palimpsest.

'When one meets one's father,' she said, 'after a long absence, whether one knows him well or not, one's heart leaps, and a great thrill strikes through one.'

'Yes,' said Frank. 'I believe my nerves would ring to the sound of my father's voice if I were hearing it, though I've never seen him.'

'Don't imagine it for a moment, dear. When your father comes back after ten years you shiver in his presence—you feel as if you had jumped into a frosty sea out of the summer. I did when I went to him from you.'

She kicked her heels against the wall, and sat on her hands, looking round and up at Frank like a bird. Then she turned her gaze into the tree. In the mood that held her, to think was to resolve. She came to her feet, and stood before her lover.

'What would you think if I were to tell you that my father had chosen a husband for me?'

'I should think it the height of folly, unless I were his selection.'

'Come to him now. Say to him that you love me, and that I love you, and that he may kill me if he likes, but that I will never marry anybody else.'

'This is encouraging.'

'And you will need courage.'

'What is wrong?'

'You'll know soon enough. Come.' And she led him to the house. She danced along the path. Her eyes clashed against his.

'I'm in the major key,' she said.

No wonder she was in the major key. She had a vision of the encounter between her lover and her father; a wordy tournament in which the former bore off the honours. Her heart was fast melting down every feeling into a glowing rage at the man who, after ten years' absence, came to blight her life; and her body, the flames about that crucible, leapt and trembled. She could move only in bounds to a measure. Frank, mystified, but flushed by sympathy, followed her, admiring.

She took him straight to the library. Lee was not there.

'Wait here, and I shall find my father,' she said.

But Miss Jane came into the room.

'How in the name of all the proprieties dare you enter this house, sir?' she cried.

Frank, as the reader will surmise, had been forbidden the house.

Muriel sat down on the couch and pulled her lover to her side. Then she rested her elbows on her knees and her chin in her hands, and looked at her aunt. It was grossly impertinent.

'For shame! What is the meaning of this folly, Muriel?' and the angry lady crossed the floor, and bristled before the couple with only a yard between.

Muriel became absolutely but serenely rabid.

'Mr. Hay is going to take supper with us to-night,' she said. 'Ring the bell please, aunt, and order supper to be hastened.'

Miss Jane towered, physically and morally.

'Muriel'—she spoke solemnly, as became her exaltation—'you wicked girl! You have much greater cause to keep your room and cry over your misdemeanours, than come here outraging all decency in this way. Have you no maidenly reserve at all?'

Then she leant towards Frank.

'Mr. Hay, I should think this exhibition of temper and impudence will make it needless to fear that you will aid further in thwarting our intentions with regard to Muriel. Indeed, I don't know at present how it will be possible for me to stand by quietly and see any young man, however eligible, throw himself away on such an incorrigible young woman.'

Thoroughly on fire at the imperturbable smile on Muriel's face, she leaned towards her again, a flaming tower of Pisa.

'Muriel, if ever you wish to regain the place you have lost in my esteem, you will tell Mr. Hay to leave this house at once, and never enter it again.'

Muriel fumbled in her pocket, and half-withdrew her hand, but thought better of it.

Miss Jane again menaced Frank.

'Mr. Hay, the cool effrontery you display in sitting quietly smiling—don't try to hide it, sir!—while the woman you profess to love throws to the winds all respect for herself and her betters, actually and openly defying her aunt——'

Muriel had risen, and was approaching the bell-pull. Her hand was almost on it, when her aunt, with surprising agility, intercepted her.

'Not while I live!' she cried, almost hysterically.

Frank rose, and began, 'I shall not——'

'You shall!' cried Muriel.

'Leave the room, Muriel!' said Miss Jane, collecting her dignity, and posing again as a tower.

Muriel's hand slipped back to her pocket, and she looked straight into her aunt's eyes. Once more she changed her purpose, and left the room with a smile, and an airy nod to Frank.

'Did that girl wink just now, sir?' said Miss Jane.

'I didn't observe.'

The excited lady pulled a chair before Frank, and sat down opposite him. 'Mr. Hay,' she said, 'I wish to be reasonable. I know myself what it is to be young. Indeed, putting other circumstances aside, I can almost sympathise with you in your infatuation for Muriel. She is really a very good-looking girl; but this scene must have convinced you that her nature is wholly unregenerate, and I hope——'

What she hoped can only be guessed, for Muriel re-entered the room.

Miss Jane rose, this time in cathedral-like grandeur. Alas! she was a very weak-tempered woman. The cathedral brought forth a cat.

'What brings you back?' she cried. 'You are a disgrace to your sex: you are no lady; you are a shameless minx!'

Muriel came close to her, her hand clutched in her pocket.

'Aunt,' she said, 'you are carrying this a little too far. Did you really suppose that I had gone at your command?'

'I certainly did; and I repeat it. Go!'

'When I leave this room, Frank goes with me. Supper will be served in a minute for him and me in my sitting-room.'

'Is it you or I that's dreaming, girl?'

'You have been dreaming, but you're wakening now. You thought you could mistress me; you can't.'

'If I can't mistress yon, as you vulgarly say, we'll see whom the servants will obey.'

Miss Jane rang the bell violently.

Muriel's hand was again half-out of her pocket, but a whimsical expression came over her face, and she returned it.

'They shan't get the chance of disobeying you,' she said, going out of the room and holding the door shut. Her aunt tried to pull it open, but did not prosecute her attempt. It was too like a school-girl. She appealed to Frank tacitly. He shook his head. To tell the truth, the young man enjoyed it rather than not.

Shortly, a housemaid's voice was heard saying, 'Supper's just ready, Miss Muriel.'

The answer came, 'Very well; that's all,' and Muriel re-entered. She put her back against the door in a blaze of triumph, and said mock-heroically, 'No one shall leave this room till supper's served.'

Miss Jane was beaten, and Muriel had conquered without it; but now she held it out, and shook it open, remorselessly, her poor, little, crumpled letter. Her aunt, who had forgotten all about it, sank on the couch sobbing hysterically. Youth will exact the uttermost farthing, knowing not how it will need much mercy itself. The girl was punished there and then by a shade that passed over her lover's brow. She felt that he remembered the scene of the discovery, and contrasted it with this; but before she had decided what amends to make Lee entered the room. He looked about him, and immediately appeared to be in a tremendous passion; Miss Jane sat up; and Muriel, crossing the floor, took Frank's arm.

'Muriel,' said Lee, 'go to your room.'

She clung to Frank.

'I never bid twice,' and he pulled her away and swung her to the door.

'This is too much!' cried Frank, stepping towards Lee.

'Mr. Hay, I suppose. I shall speak with you immediately.'

Muriel was about to approach Frank again, but Lee pointed her sternly to the door. As before, in his presence, and by his conduct, she was utterly bewildered, and wandered out of the room as if she had lost her wits.

'Here's a change!' exclaimed Miss Jane, 'What a disgraceful scene there has been here, brother! I apologise to myself for allowing my emotions to overcome me.'

'Leave us, please, Jane.'

'Certainly, Henry,' and as she went, she cast a withering look at Frank.

CHAPTER VI

LEE ENJOYS HIMSELF

Lee sat down behind the table and began to point a quill. Frank took a chair opposite him.

'Mr. Hay,' said Lee, 'we may as well come to the point at once. My daughter cannot marry you. I have chosen her a husband.'

'I am glad to come to the point at once,' said Frank. 'Miss Chartres bade me tell you that she will have no husband but me. She sends you this message: You may kill her, but you cannot force her to marry against her will.'

'I am sorry her message is so commonplace. It indicates that her novel-reading has not been eclectic, to say the least; and, which is of more importance to me, it lowers the tone of the present work. That, of course, you don't understand; but no matter. Force her to marry against her will? Surely not. *You* know, if *she* doesn't, that people never act against their wills. We will change her will, or kill it.'

'Which would be to kill her.'

'I'm not so sure of that. It will be an interesting experiment. I understand you to say that by the time my daughter's will has been conquered, her body must be so reduced that death will ensue. Now, I do not think so. What will you wager that she does not survive the subjugation of her will?'

There was a pause before Frank replied, which gave his answer an appearance of deliberation it did not possess. He was so astonished at the beaming satisfaction on Lee's face, utterly incompatible under any hypothesis he could think of, with the cold-blooded, heartless suggestion regarding Muriel, that words were denied him for a second or two. When they did come, slowly and vehemently, they had more reference to the character of the wagerer than the matter of the villainous bet.

'You are a scoundrel!'

Lee laid down the quill with which he had been dallying, and settled himself comfortably in his chair. He expected to derive great pleasure from this interview. Hitherto he had been dealing with women and servants; he was now to have a foeman worthy of his steel.

'I am a scoundrel,' he said, weighing each word. 'That is your position. Now, how will you defend it?'

The momentary blankness on Frank's face made Lee fear he had been too precipitate, and had routed the young man with this wholly unexpected turn, putting an end to the intellectual enjoyment he had anticipated. So when the blankness left Frank's face, the child-like happiness which dwelt in every line of Lee's could only be matched by the pictured countenance of some rapt and smiling medieval saint. The young man, concluding that he had to deal with what the world calls a 'character,' met him on his own ground.

'Your imperturbability under the accusation is the best proof, I think.' He said this mildly and collectedly, not wishing to give Lee the advantage of his coolness.

'A very fair answer,' said Lee. 'I shall allow you this stroke by way of compensation. Poor fellow, you will have a sore heart for a while, I imagine. You're not a fool, and you're good-looking. I think more of my daughter on your account.'

Lee resumed the quill, and began to write with a perfect assumption of unconcern. Frank stood up, put both hands on the table, leant forward a little, and delivered himself of a short speech. His blood was up, and he spoke very little above a whisper.

'Mr. Chartres, you have the right to control the actions of your daughter. You are going to abuse that right. I shall interfere. Your daughter loves me; you are going to force her from me; I shall do all I can to prevent you. I love your daughter; I shall stick at nothing to obtain her: Mr. Chartres, I shall succeed.'

The practical novelist positively trembled with delight.

'I like you, young man,' he cried; 'and I believe you will improve. I think you will be unconsciously my best collaborateur. Both your character and Muriel's will be tested, illuminated, and strengthened for good or evil, in the course of this work, and that immediately. Who would write who has once tasted the pleasures of this new fiction! This is a foreign language to you. Some day I may teach you its whole secret. In the meantime regard me as a student of character, who, tired of books, of the dead subject, has taken to vivisection—vivisection of the soul. Well, sir, it is to be a duel, then. Good. I have a suspicion you imagine it is your bold bearing that makes me so placid. You are mistaken. It is my habit in opposition. I learnt it in the jungle, shooting tigers. My gun is always heavily loaded. I take a deliberate aim. If I shoot a tiger, it is killed; if a turtle-dove, it is blown to pieces. You comprehend.'

'Me, the turtle-dove; yes. And the bereaved mate will peck herself to death,' said Frank with considerable coolness.

'In a cage we can force her to live,' said Lee.

Frank had thought to meet Lee on his own ground, but found himself wholly at sea. He would strike out boldly till he touched land again.

'I am astonished,' he said, 'that a man like you, who seem to trample on conventionalities should arrogate to himself that absurd authority claimed by some fathers over the hands of their daughters.'

'And what if it were because parental jurisdiction over marriage is becoming a thing of the past that I make myself absolute?'

'That would be very foolish,' said Frank, forgetting with whom he was dealing.

'That is no argument, my good sir,' came from Lee at once, and Frank saw his mistake.

'You see,' continued Lee, 'the idea of the parent is changing. The popular parent is the servant of his children. Now, whenever an idea, an opinion—a song, a faith, a show—becomes popular, I know at once it has some inherent weakness, some hollow lie; for the world is weak and false, and all kinds of froth and flame commend themselves to it. An opinion is like a jug of beer: the foaming head attracts the youth; the old toper blows it off.'

'You think yourself clever, but this is rank sophistry.'

'No argument again. Go away, Mr. Hay, and learn to do something besides assert. Come back and have a talk as soon as you really have something to say.'

Frank walked slowly to the door. He was endeavouring to estimate Lee. Did all fathers treat unsuitable candidates for their daughters' hands to such a dose of brusque philosophy? Surely not. Then, did all fathers returned from India with dark skins, and, presumably, no livers, behave in this fashion? He could not believe it. He returned to the charge.

'Why are you so ill-bred?' he asked.

'I am not ill-bred. Had I received you with anything but a downright refusal your hopes would have risen. Had I agreed with you in anything, you would have thought, "I may manage him yet." I have been kind to you. I have been most polite. I have not deceived you for an instant. Do not think that the suave manner is the sign of the kind heart. What is called politeness is, as you know, the commonest form of hypocrisy; courtesy has become etiquette, and the gentleman is the ghost of a dead chivalry.'

'You are a braggart as well as a sophist. You——'

'Go away till you learn to do other than assert and call names.'

'I will speak. You said a little while ago that when an opinion became popular, you, in effect, adopted its converse.'

'Too hard and fast; but go on.'

'Marriage is coming to be regarded more and more as a mere civil relation; you will, I have no doubt, look upon it as a sacred thing. If the heart does not go along with a holy ordinance, it is the blackest sin to take part in it. Will you play the devil to your own daughter?'

'Ah, this is better!' said Lee with glistening eyes. 'In the same way any marriage not consented to by the woman's father must be unholy also. Two evils you see.'

'Who can doubt which is the less?'

'Now you are the sophist. There is no less or greater evil; it is all tarred with the same stick. But, to take a broader view. I firmly believe that marriages are made in heaven; therefore I should suppose, a marriage as ordained by heaven, happens once in fifty years, and it seems to me as likely that the decree of fate would be fulfilled in the father's choice as in the daughter's; and much more so when the father is a past master in the study of character.'

Frank was exasperated.

'Have you no heart?' he said.

The smile on Lee's face told him what a commonplace he had uttered. Smothering his emotion, he said, 'You teach me how to think and how to act. Marriages *are* made in heaven, and you were not married. If you had been you would have loved your daughter. A man of your no-principles must be answered as the fool is—according to his folly. And indeed you are a kind of fool, and a bad kind. I said before, thoughtlessly, that I would stick at nothing in endeavouring to make Miss Chartres my wife. Now I repeat it with full purpose.'

'Good,' said Lee, rubbing his hands. 'Still a little too much nicknaming, but, on the whole, good. You are a capital collaborateur. I have taught you how to think and act already. Are you not astonished at yourself? What would they think at your debating club of this talk of ours? If you like it, come back and have some more.'

Frank went to the door in silence, but returned again.

'Ah!' exclaimed Lee. '"He often took leave, but was loath to depart!" What! Is it meant to be considered by me evidence of your determined spirit? Eh? Is it a dodge?'

'Ill-doers are ill-dreaders,' said Frank. 'I am not going to speak for myself, but for Muriel. You have talked of her as if she were a thing that you could turn to any use, and you have spoken of caging her. I perceive you to be most irrational and obstinate. I can imagine your going great lengths to obtain a desired end. Promise me that you will not use physical force in any——'

'I never make promises.'

'Then,' pursued Frank in a tone of entreaty that had mastered his voice to his great annoyance, for he felt that it was enjoyed like a sacrifice by the apparently infernal spirit whom he addressed—'I demand to know what weapons you will use. Will you employ force?'

'I am always armed to the teeth.'

'You mean you are unscrupulous.'

'Yes.'

'It is impossible to reason with you, I defy you. Why, you are an insolent, cold-blooded villain, and deserve a horsewhipping.'

'I will take an early opportunity of presenting you with a horsewhip to attempt the administration of one,' said Lee with perfect good humour.

'Let it be very soon,' said Frank, going, 'for when you are my father-in-law I will decline the offer.'

Lee rose to his feet. 'You wish this colloquy to end theatrically,' he said. 'I will disappoint you. You may marry my daughter, if you can.'

CHAPTER VII

THE UNEXPECTED

Muriel had bribed the servant who should have shown Frank out to bring him to her sitting-room; and this was accomplished without observation. As he entered, Muriel's appearance astonished him. She looked superb in his eyes—flushed, bright, bold, a wonderful contrast to the haggard girl Lee had hurled from him half an hour before. The momentary defeated feeling was past. She now stood on her rights. No father or man should have treated her as Lee had done, and she replied by sticking to her purpose, and having Frank sup with her.

'Sit, sit,' she said. 'We'll not say a word about anything until we've supped—I mean about anything except the supper.'

They were both very hungry, and on the principle that promptitude in action is the best prayer for the success of any enterprise, dispensed with a grace. Truly, the good eater, if he masticate well, renders the best thanks. Frank and Muriel worshipped God heartily before the great mahogany altar of Britain—which was in this instance, a little one of walnut—rapidly replacing the mercy of appetite by the mercy of satisfaction.

Meantime Lee had other visitors. Mr. Linty, the family lawyer, succeeded Frank almost immediately, and Miss Jane accompanied him into the library. Lee knew about him from some of the letters he had read. He was, however, wholly unprepared to enter into business with him; but pleasure he expected.

After the formal courtesies, the lawyer began. He was a sandy-haired, little, dry, old gentleman, and spoke very stiffly.

'Mr. Chartres,' he said, 'the intent with which I visit you to-day is to convey to you certain information which I think it my duty to let you have as soon as possible.'

'I am a man of business,' said Lee.

'Good, sir; very good. Mr. Chartres, an entailed estate is in a most delicate position, surrounded as it is with innumerable statutory provisions. It is doubtful whether you would be able, supposing you were so inclined, to make good a claim on Snell without proving the death of your brother Robert.'

Imagining that the lawyer had made a mistake in using Robert instead of William, and that there had been circumstances in connection with the death of the late proprietor which he had not learned; wishing, besides, to gain time, as this was the first intimation he had received of the estate being entailed, Lee said in a half-bantering tone, 'Well, you know, I never had a brother, Robert.'

'O!' said the lawyer.

'Well,' began Miss Jane, but stopped short, not sure what to say or think.

Lee surpassed himself at this juncture. Not a feature of his face showed he was at a loss. He turned to Miss Jane and asked in a sort of parenthesis, 'What were you going to say?'

'O!' said Miss Jane, 'I think, and I always told William, that although nothing has been heard of Robert for thirty years, he may still be alive. William said that he died to the family when he became a prodigal, and forbade his name to be mentioned. I thought that uncharitable.'

'Ay,' said Lee indifferently. 'Of course, I agreed with William.'

It was very successful.

'But,' said Mr. Linty, 'We *must* speak of him, for, if he is alive the estate is his. Do you know anything of him?'

'No,' said Lee; 'but as we have not heard of him for thirty years, we may reasonably suppose him dead.'

'By no means. That cannot even be taken as presumptive evidence. If there were seventy years from the birth of your brother there would be no difficulty, but if he is alive he will only be fifty-five. I am afraid the estate will require to be "hung up"—put into the hands of trustees.'

'Well, sir,' said Lee, rising, 'your contribution to this work is wholly unexpected, but likely to produce most interesting complications. I am indeed much obliged to you. There is nothing original in it, but a missing heir is a very good thing to fall back on.'

The lawyer, supposing he had heard an elaborate, and, if so, certainly incomprehensible joke, laughed appreciatively. Miss Jane frowned and examined Lee all over with scorn and minuteness.

The latter continued. 'You must really excuse me just now. I only reached Snell House a few hours ago, and I am in no condition to discuss business. I suppose,' with a laugh, 'you won't turn us out immediately.'

'By no means,' said Mr. Linty. 'In all likelihood there will be no need for that. I shall expect a visit from you to-morrow. Good evening.'

Miss Jane, who was a great friend of Mr. Linty's, left the library to see him to the door.

Lee's next visitor was of a different quality. He was an old man, very ill-dressed, the great size of his head, which was covered with thick white hair, being the most notable thing about him. Miss Jane introduced him, having met him at the door when she parted with the lawyer.

'This is Clacher, brother,' she said. 'You remember it was he who found William's body on the road.'

Lee did remember, as it had been mentioned in one of the letters he had read. Miss Jane informed Lee further under her breath, that Clacher was quite mad, although harmless, and that he got a living by begging in the disguise of a hawker. He had called often since the death of William, asking for the 'new Mr. Chartres.'

'I am very glad you have brought him to me,' said Lee. 'He may be useful.'

He then advanced to the old pedlar, and held out his hand, saying, 'How do you do, Mr. Clacher?'

Clacher emitted a chuckling noise, and darted glances at odd corners of the room—glances which, if it had been possible to enclose them, would have been found to resemble blind alleys, as they ran a certain distance into space and stopped without lighting on anything. Then he said in a hoarse, harsh voice, speaking to himself as much as to Lee, 'I'm gaun tae dae it Englified.'

He pulled himself up with all the appearance of a man about to make a lengthy statement; but instead of a speech he only succeeded in a pitiful pantomimic display. He could not remember what he had come to say. As if to stir up his dormant faculties he began rubbing his head with both hands, gathering his thick hair into shocks, and then scattering these asunder. While endeavouring to make hay of his hair in this manner, his little fierce eyes, like swivel-guns of exceedingly minute calibre, resumed firing their blank shots into space. Then, satisfied apparently that nothing could be done toward the tedding of his hair, he rubbed his shaved cheeks, beat his forehead and his breast, and tore at the fingers of both hands.

All at once he stood erect, and, as if he were resuming a train of thought, or a conversation, said, 'It's a wonnerfu' secret.'

'Indeed?' said Lee, quietly.

'Ay; for it can pit another in the deid man's shoes ye stann' in. But I was gaun tae dae it Englified. Ye micht check me when I gang wrang.'

'Check you when you go wrong?'

'That's it! "Go wrong"—no, "gang wrang." Keep me richt—right, will you, sir?'

'It's of no consequence to me, my good man,' replied Lee, 'whether you speak Englified as you call it, or not; but I'll keep you right if you like.'

'Thank you, thank you! But whaat———'

'What,' said Lee.

'Bide a wee, bide a wee!' cried Clacher, rubbing his hair.

'Ye see,' he continued, 'if I tak' time tae dae it Englified, I forget it. Whaat wis it I wis gaun tae dae Englified, and whaat for wis I gaun to dae it Englified? I canna' mind, I canna' mind.'

'Never mind, then,' said Lee, gently. 'You interest me as much as any character in the story. It seems indeed to be made to my hand, and I shall only require to mould it here and there in order to give it distinction.'

'Ye're mad, ye're mad!' cried Clacher, excitedly, shaking his big frowsy head, and seeing Lee for the first time, although his eyes had seemed fixed on him repeatedly.

'Poor fellow!' said Lee to Miss Jane, 'he thinks everybody mad but himself, like all lunatics.'

'Lunatics,' said Miss Jane, emphatically, 'are unerring judges of the lunacy of others.'

'I've heard that, too,' said Lee, ingenuously.

'My good friend,' he continued, addressing Clacher, 'we must really try and remember what and why it is to be done Englified. Come with me and you shall have something to eat and a glass of good wine. If that doesn't startle your memory I don't know what will.'

Miss Jane looked volumes, but only said, 'Henry, there never was a man so changed as you.'

'My dear Jane,' said Lee, 'in ten years—why, I might have become a lunatic too.'

As he crossed the hall with Clacher to the dining-room, a sound of laughter from upstairs struck on his ear. He stopped, and listened. It was repeated, and the laughing voices were Muriel's and another's. Entering the dining-room he hastily confided Clacher to the care of Briscoe and Dempster, who were discussing a bottle of port, and hurried away to Muriel's sitting-room. He went in without knocking, and another peal of laughter came to an early death. Frank and Muriel stood up as the door opened. She meant to fight;

he recognised the falseness of their position, and felt, as he looked, exceedingly awkward.

'Father,' began Muriel, looking in Lee's direction, but past him, through the open door, 'you must not——'

She got no further; for she saw coming towards her room, in single file, Miss Jane, Dempster, Briscoe, and Clacher. It is pretty certain that none of these four persons knew exactly why they had come upstairs. Miss Jane probably expected some kind of scene to take place at which she might have an interest in assisting; Dempster followed her out of sheer stupidity; Briscoe came after Dempster because he was drunk; and Clacher after him because he was mad, and didn't know any better. When Miss Jane, arriving at the top of the staircase, saw Muriel's door open, she hesitated; but behind her there came such a motley procession that she had to go on. She stopped at the door; the others stood about her in a semi-circle, and the *tableau* was complete.

Lee, the only individual of the seven who was thoroughly collected, said, looking round him meditatively, 'The situation is turning out better than it promised to. After all, what more can we do either in writing fiction or creating it than follow an indication, and let the rest come.'

He then motioned Miss Jane aside and, taking Briscoe's hand, led him into the room. The maudlin gravity with which that worthy bore himself, combined with a remarkable bulging about the pockets, made him a very comic figure, and raised a smile even on Muriel's face. But Lee took one of her hands and put it in one of Briscoe's, saying, 'Muriel, this is your future husband.'

She turned very pale; and almost fainted, when a hazy smile struggled into Briscoe's slack mouth and dull eyes, and he attempted to kiss her. She broke from him with a half-suppressed exclamation of disgust, and would have thrown her arms round Frank; but Lee seized her, and handed her over to her aunt who had entered the room.

'Leave my house,' he then said to Frank, with a gesture of authority.

It was a peculiar position for the young man, and Lee watched him with intense interest. Frank walked to Muriel, kissed her on the cheek, whispered something in her ear, and then passed out through the little crowd at the door without looking to the right hand or the left.

'Very good!' exclaimed Lee. 'Perhaps that's the best thing he could have done.'

'But, Henry,' said Miss Jane, 'I think Mr. Dempster would like to marry Muriel.'

'Me!' shouted Dempster spirally. 'No; I assure you. My dear Miss Jane, I would as soon think of marrying you. Eh—ah—I mean well.'

Miss Jane's face quivered a second, but she said nothing, and left the room. Dempster, aghast at his dreadful mistake, followed her downstairs. Clacher, unable to make up his mind whether to stick by Briscoe or follow Dempster, sat down disconsolately on the top step, with his elbows on his knees and his head between his hands. Lee also went out, signing to Briscoe to follow him. Then Lee locked Muriel into her room, and putting the key in his pocket, took Briscoe and Clacher to the library with him.

It was half-past nine when Muriel found herself a prisoner; and Frank had whispered that he would wait for her all night at the low wall.

CHAPTER VIII

BRISCOE SEES THINGS IN A NEW LIGHT

Food and drink were provided for Clacher in the library. It was a very large room, and he sat at a little table in the corner, out of hearing of the low tones in which Briscoe and Lee conversed.

Lee was exceedingly angry at Briscoe for having got tipsy, and rated him severely, getting no response, however, save laughter or a drunken 'You shut up.' At last, losing patience, he dashed a tumbler of water in the drunken man's face. Briscoe rose to strike; but Lee gave him another tumbler, and while he was still rubbing the water out of his eyes, a third, which knocked him down into his chair again, pretty well sobered and very surly. Lee was a man of great physical strength, and although on several occasions Briscoe had been able to control his will, a single bout at fisticuffs had shown, once for all, who was master in that branch of dialectic.

'My dear Briscoe,' said Lee, handing him his handkerchief to help to dry himself, 'this is really too bad of you. Do you think I don't know the meaning of those stuffed pockets of yours? You've been helping yourself, forgetting altogether the work of art in which we are engaged.'

'Heaven helps those that help themselves,' growled Briscoe, still a little maudlin and very crusty.

'A very good proverb indeed; but it has always seemed to me to require a gloss, as, say, "Help yourself, and Heaven will develop heroic qualities in you by opposing you." So you see I am interfering with you to give your acts a higher tone. You'll have to empty out your pockets, my boy. Nobody need know; and, if they should, kleptomania is quite genteel.'

'Now, look here,' said Briscoe: 'I'm not fit for this almighty art of yours. By Jove, when I think of where I am, and what we're up to, I can hardly believe it's me! Just you give me as much money as you can, and let me slope quietly, and you'll get on far better without me. I never could grease myself and worm through the tight places—get through the world, as folks say; and I tell you it would be far better for you if I were away.'

'Briscoe, I have always admired your independent character,' said Lee. 'Neither can I get through the world; but there's another method which equally insures success, and that is, to transcend the world: death by starvation is then itself a glorious triumph—the triumph of the idea. I know what I mean, and, though I were to explain till doomsday, you wouldn't, so it don't matter. You will confer a lasting benefit on the world if you stay and help with the work in which I am engaged. It is a glorious labour, apart from its artistic merit; for it is raising the tone of everybody about me. It is just what these people needed, especially Muriel and Frank—the dash of bitter that strengthens the sweet, the need for rebellion that wakens the soul, the spur that drives natures roughshod over convention, the——'

'Draw it mild,' interposed Briscoe sneeringly. 'To-morrow, or maybe to-night, Caroline will be down with the real man, and what will you do then?'

'I long for their arrival. That will be the great scene.'

'What'll you do?'

'Well, murder I merely glanced at. To turn them out of the house as impostors, though a simple solution of the matter for a short time, would only stave off a final settlement. This is what I intend: to shut up Chartres in one of the rooms, pinioned, and, if necessary, gagged, as a dangerous lunatic, until I can have him removed to a private asylum, which will be a matter of only a few hours; and, once there, we are safer than if he were in the grave.'

'How will you manage that?'

'The simplest thing in the world. You can't have read many novels or you wouldn't ask. Besides the novels, however, I have studied the lunacy laws; and I could put you, Briscoe—sensible, hard-headed fellow as you are—into an asylum to-morrow, and defy the world to take you out!'

'By Jove, there's a chance here!' said Briscoe. 'Damn it, man, banish your dreams, and do the thing as a downright piece of the finest villainy ever perpetrated.'

'I haven't the least objection, my dear Briscoe, that you should be a villain. There's not one, at present, in the work, and if you choose, still collaborating with me, to adopt such a role, I shall be very glad indeed.'

'I'll do it,' said Briscoe, rising. 'I'll go off to Glasgow and prepare the whole thing for to-morrow early.'

'The last train from Greenock left some time ago.'

'What! is it so late as that?'

'Yes; but you can go off to-morrow before breakfast.'

'Very well. But we're going to do this, mind! No shamming—no artistic flourishes—upright, downright villainy!'

'On your part, certainly.'

'And I'm to marry Muriel?'

'Oh, you must see that is impossible. The girl will fight to the death against it. Besides, it would be thoroughly inartistic. No, no. My intention is to bring about an elopement; and then to discover that you are Frank's father. You see? You're old enough. He's only twenty-two, and you're over forty. The invention of antecedents and the getting up evidence will be most engrossing. Of course I'll intercept these young people, and drive them to the very last resource. It will do them any amount of good.'

Briscoe put up his hand warningly, and Lee turned his head and saw Clacher standing behind him.

'Ah! my good friend,' he said, 'have you had enough?'

'Ay,' said Clacher.

'Do you remember what it is you want to do "Englified"?'

'No—yet.'

'Do you think you'll remember soon?'

'Mebbe, if ye'll let me alone, and gie me some mair drink. Whusky.'

'Certainly,' said Lee, rising. 'You can have this room to yourself, and I shall send you whiskey.'

'I think I'll go to bed,' said Briscoe. 'I'm very tired; and I'll have an early start to-morrow.'

'Come out and smoke a cigar with me first,' said Lee. And then in a whisper, 'I want you to help me. They may arrive any moment.'

'Of course,' replied Briscoe, in the same tone, clenching his fists. 'I forgot that.'

So Clacher was left with a decanter of whiskey; and as soon as he was alone he pulled from his breast-pocket a dirty letter, which he read and re-read, and thought over and got madder about: and he always took the other glass of whiskey, muttering to himself, 'I canna' mind, I canna' mind.'

CHAPTER IX

DEMPSTER APOLOGISES

While Briscoe was being sobered in the library a remarkable scene transacted itself in the dining-room between Miss Jane and Dempster. The outraged lady settled herself in an easy chair with a book; but the offender entered before she had time to read six lines. He approached her on tip-toe, and, a spring seeming to give way somewhere within him, he came down plump on one knee, as if he had been a puppet, and burst out woefully 'Eh—ah!' like an escape of saw-dust.

Miss Jane ignored him, and pressed open her book, which was new and stiff.

Dempster cleared his throat of the saw-dust, and with drooping head, his left hand on his left knee and his right arm hanging limp, whispered, just above his breath, 'Miss Chartres, you see before you a miserable being.'

'I don't; I'm not looking,' said the lady sharply, disconcerting Dempster terribly.

'If you would look you would see me,' he said nervously, as several watch-springs seemed to break out of bounds in various parts of his anatomy.

Miss Jane looked over the top of her book. She saw him collapsed before her with abased eyes, and was satisfied. So she hid her face again, smiling, and said coldly, 'I have seen you.'

'Have you?' said Dempster, going off, as it were accidentally, like a gun; 'I'm very glad: for I would have had no rest of mind or body if you hadn't looked at me. I would have gone about like a hen that had lost her—I mean——'

'Well, and say ill, Mr. Dempster,' said Miss Jane, unable to resist the chance which she had long desired to take. 'These kind of people often make more mischief than ill-doers,' she added.

This overwhelmed Dempster. Down he came on the other knee, and, clasping both hands, called out in serpentine anguish, and without a stammer, 'Why are you so hard on me? The moment I made that unfortunate remark about marrying you, the earth, the sun, my wealth, and life and death were to me no more than they are to a poor man. I assure you, I assure you—I don't exaggerate; and I beg you, I implore you to forgive me.'

'Rise, Mr. Dempster,' said Miss Jane with a slight return of graciousness. 'There is really nothing to forgive.'

Some automatic winding-up process began within him and would soon have brought him to his feet with a bound, but Miss Jane's reply to his 'And we will be friends as we were before?' made him all run down again; for the lady said, 'That can hardly be. Though mistakes may not require forgiveness, they cannot always be forgotten. But rise, please.'

'I'll not rise till you forget,' said Dempster with pitiful resignation, his various members barely hanging together. The poor fellow was in deader earnest than even Miss Jane supposed, as will shortly appear.

'But I cannot forget,' said the lady. 'Thought is free, and self-willed besides, Mr. Dempster.'

He clasped his hands again, and in a succession of spasms ejaculated, 'You are the only woman whose society I have any comfort in. You understand me; and your advice is always good, and—eh—ah—agreeable. You never snub me—at least not often, and not without good reason—like younger, like thoughtless hoydens. If you won't forget and be friends with me again, I don't know whatever I'm to do. I have nothing at all to think of now Muriel has rejected me; and I'll have nobody I can talk to with any frankness if you go on remembering.'

Miss Jane's blood, which was not by any means a meagre decoction, but on the contrary rich and sweet enough yet, tingled to her finger ends. This man actually needed her! She laid aside her book, leant forward a little, resting her hands neatly in her lap. There was no smile, but she looked with a gentle earnestness, and the tang was gone from her tongue.

'How am I to forget?' she said. 'Tell me that, and I'll try. I suppose you have not forgotten what you said—very bitter words for any woman to digest. You would as soon think of marrying me as of marrying a young hoyden, who, from what I can make out, had just rejected you with insult; and the tone of voice—the tone of voice! But rise, Mr. Dempster.'

'I won't,' he said, looking her right in the face, and wondering that he had never noticed before how silky her brown hair was, and how kindly her brown eyes. 'I won't. Forget and then I'll rise.'

'How can I forget?' softly.

'Just as easily as I can rise. The mind is like legs; it can be bent and unbent.'

Now Miss Jane was not very much of a prude; but Dempster was becoming too confident. He must be brought low again. So she lifted her book and said 'Shocking!'

'I beg your pardon,' he cried, vexed at finding the stumbling-block, which he had nearly rolled up to the top and kicked over the other side out of sight for ever, down at the bottom of the hill again. 'I didn't mean to say,' trying to twist his fingers into a hay-band, 'that your mind was like my legs—oh dear me! I've put both feet in it now!'

Miss Jane hid her face completely, but it was to conceal a smile.

Dempster smoothed his cheeks with both hands and held his head for a second or two, all of him gathered up in a more powerful effort to think than he had ever made in his life before.

'What can I do to make you forget?' he muttered.

'Ah!' he cried, after a second, pulling the book from Miss Jane's face as a child might have done, 'I think I'm going to have an idea.'

'You don't mean to say so!' said Miss Jane, leaning forward again in the same neat, pleasant way, with a laugh that was almost girlish.

'Yes, I believe I am,' said Dempster, sitting down on the calves of his legs with his hands on his knees, and looking up trustfully, like something in india-rubber.

'If I were to say,' he enunciated slowly, 'something contradicting emphatically what you can't at present forget, you might—eh—ah—forget?'

'Yes.'

He had been about a foot from her, and he now scraped along the ground on his knees until he almost touched hers.

'You might try to say something of that kind,' she said, blushing, and with a little gasp. Now that it seemed to be coming she was put out; but, like a brave woman having her last chance, she kept her position and smiled encouragingly.

'Might I? Oh, thank you!' he cried with effusion.

Then he knitted his brows and rubbed his head. His serpentine faculty was in abeyance—these involuntaries of his had to cease in order that he might once in his life attempt to think.

As for Miss Jane, she was mistaken in imagining that he had the least notion of making love to her. He valued her only as a friend, and had splashed into the quicksand of a proposal of marriage without knowing it. She thought, however, that he only needed a touch to make him bury himself, like a flounder, head over ears in a declaration of love and an offer of his hand and heart; so she gave him that touch softly and sweetly.

'You said,' quoth she, 'with the utmost disdain, that you would as soon think of marrying me as my insolent niece.'

'I did, I did. Can you help me to contradict it emphatically?'

'I'm afraid not—dear Mr. Dempster.'

'Eh?' said he. 'Thank you.'

He felt dimly that there was something in the air—dimly, as protoplasm may feel its existence.

'Ah!' he cried. 'Here's a kind of notion. I wonder if it's an idea. Would it do to say, in order to make you forget, just the opposite of what I said? You see—you understand—something like this, meaning—of course, you know what I mean—nothing more, you know—eh—ah!—suppose I say, "I would far rather marry you than Muriel." Is that—emphatic enough?'

Miss Jane bent forward, and put her head on his left shoulder, and her hand on his right.

'Mr. Dempster!' she said. 'Alec!' she sighed.

'Eh?—eh—ah!'—and he had to hold her—to clutch her, to save himself from falling.

'I'm the happiest woman in the world.'

'I'm—I'm very glad of it.'

'I never loved anybody before,' she said, so sweetly that Dempster wondered.

Then she buried her face in his neck, she did, the stupid, soft-hearted creature, and whispered, 'Oh, the torture of wooing you for Muriel! But now I have my reward!'

And she did think this as she said it, although it had never occurred to her before.

'Yes,' said Dempster, feeling that the pause must be filled up somehow. 'Of course,' he added, making a half-hearted attempt to force her back into her chair, which she mistook for a caress, 'I only suggested the contradiction. I did not——'

But her eyes were shut, and her brain too.

'I adore your modesty,' she whispered. 'Trust me, trust me. I will love you till death.'

'I'm completely stumped,' exclaimed Dempster.

'Poor dear!' said Miss Jane, mistaking. And, indeed it was pardonable, Dempster's metaphors being usually marked by a *curiosa infelicitas*.

Here the door opened briskly and Mrs. Cherry, the housekeeper, burst into the room.

'Losh me! Miss Chartres!' she cried, as the pair scrambled to their feet.

'Mrs. Cherry,' said Miss Jane, with great presence of mind, in spite of a distinct tremor in her voice, 'since you have seen, I may as well tell you. Mr. Dempster is going to marry me. But why did you come in without knocking, and what do you want?'

Mrs. Cherry made a dreadful mess of her story. It will be clearer to the reader in a form different from that which she gave to it.

The housekeeper's room was on the ground floor, and directly under Muriel's sitting-room. About half-past nine Mrs. Cherry's gossip, Mrs. Shaw, dropped in for a chat. These two good women were widows of fifty, and whatever their talk began with, it usually ended in laudation of their sainted husbands. The crack reached that stage about ten o'clock on the night of our story, and Mrs. Shaw's panegyric was soon in full blast.

'Maister Shaw,' she said, twiddling her thumbs, 'wis a fine man. The cliverest, godliest, brawest Christian, an' a gentleman though he merrit me. He could write, ay, an' coont, mind ye, for a' the warl' as weel as ony bairn o' fourteen in thae' days when a'body's brats gang to the schule. An' for readin'—losh, wumman!—he would sit glowerin' at a pipper a nicht wi' the interestedest look in his een—sae dwamt-like that ye wad hae' thocht he didna' ken a word.'

'What's that?' said Mrs. Cherry, starting in her chair.

'What's what?' said Mrs. Shaw.

'I thocht I heard a scart at the windy, an' somethin' gie a saft thump on the gravel.'

'Ne'er a bit o't. Some maukin loupin' alang, or mebbe a rotten or a moosie clawin' in the wa' tae let us ken it's time we were beddit, and the hoose quate, for it tae come oot an' pike the crumbs on the flare, an toast its bit broon back in the ase. I mind fine sitting at oor ingle ae Januwar nicht wi' Maister Shaw. He had a pipper, an' I was knittin'. There was nae soond but the wag-at-the-wa' tick-tickin', like an artifeecial cricket with the busiest, conthiest birr, an' my wairs gaun clickaty-click, when I heard a cheep, cheep. Maister Shaw an' me lookit up thegither, an' there we saw, sittin' on the bar fornent the emp'y side—for the chimbley was that big we aye keepit a fire in the half o't only—the gauciest, birkiest, sleekest wratch o' a moose, cockin' its roon' pukit lugs, an' keekin' by the corners o' naethin' wi' its bit pints o' een. By-an'-bye it gied anither chirp, an' syne we heard a kin' o' a smo'ored cheepin' at the back o' the lum; an' in a gliffin' seeven wee bonny moosikies happit oot a hole that naebody wad hae' thocht o' bein' there, an' crooched in a raw, winkin' on their minnie. I lookit at Maister Shaw, an' he turn't up his een like a deid blaeck in the dumfooderdest way; an' his pipper gied the gentiest sough o' a rooshle; an' whan we lookit at the grate again we just got a glint o' the wairy tail o' the big moose weekin' intae its hole. But lord hae' mercy! What's that?'

'I tell't ye!' quoth Mrs. Cherry.

'Gosh me! There it's again!'

Twice a sound similar to that which had first startled Mrs. Cherry was repeated—a slight swish past the window, and a flop on the gravel.

The two old ladies sat with their hands clasped and their mouths open. Neither of them had the courage to pull up the blind, and watch if on a third repetition the sound should be accompanied by any sight. In a few seconds a louder, harder thud, preceded by no rubbing on the window, and followed by a noise as of some one running on the gravel, appalled the two old dames. Screaming, they flew to the kitchen, where Mrs. Cherry left her friend, and hurrying to the dining-room, in her fright threw open the door without announcing herself, and interrupted so interesting a *tete-a-tete*.

Miss Jane, by dint of interrogation and remorseless interruption, which sometimes failed in its object—that of restoring to Mrs. Cherry the thread of her story—at length understood, discarding a vast quantity of irrelevant information, that the two women had been frightened by strange noises at the window of the housekeeper's room. Shrewdly guessing as to its cause, she was proceeding with Dempster to institute a formal investigation into the mystery, when a much more incomprehensible affair met her in the hall.

This is what she saw: Lee and Briscoe carrying the body of a man—who might be dead or unconscious, and whose face was covered with a handkerchief—and followed by a tall comely woman, sobbing bitterly. They passed upstairs. Miss Jane, Dempster, and the housekeeper were still standing at the door of the dining-room, amazed and silent, when Lee came down.

'You must allow this to pass unquestioned at present,' he said loftily. 'It is a very serious and sorrowful matter, and I would prefer to explain it to-morrow.'

'Very well, Henry,' said Miss Jane, even more loftily, 'you know your own affairs best. By-the-bye,' she added, as if it were a matter of course, 'from what Mrs. Cherry tells me, I think Muriel has jumped out of the window.'

'By Jove! Where should she go?'

'To the north wall, of course.'

'To be sure.'

Snatching a riding-whip from a rack, he strode to the door, but turned and said, 'This must be left entirely to me—entirely,' he repeated as Miss Jane began to remonstrate.

She was much huffed, but withdrew into the dining-room with Dempster, and the housekeeper returned to her room.

Lee had received his first check. Hitherto everybody and everything had obeyed him; but now Briscoe had spoiled part of his plan. Briscoe's courage had soon ebbed in the coolness of the night-air, and, instead of allowing the scene to take place which Lee wished in order to justify him in having Chartres bound and gagged as a madman, he had made the latter insensible the moment he stepped out of the cab which had driven him and Caroline from Greenock. This was done with chloroform, a bottle of which he had found while rummaging through the bedroom assigned to him. Caroline he had quieted by assuring her that if she said one word of betrayal he would at once put an end to Chartres' life—a threat, which, having regard to what had already taken place, she did not care to brave.

In this way Briscoe had taken the lead, reducing Lee to the necessity of acting along with him for the nonce.

CHAPTER X

THE NIGHT BREEZE

Frank sat on the north wall watching the moon through the leaves. Her light was faint, for the skirts of the day still swept the west. He had watched her for half an hour—the pale crescent, which even in that short time had seemed to wane, as her light waxed and her horns grew keener on the night's front—the high forlorn hope of heaven's host that could not all that month drive out the day. He sat under the close silence of the elm, among whose leaves there crept the faint, veiled murmur of the seaboard, fingered by the brooding surges as they beat out their slow, uncertain, soft-swelling music. Now and again there came, twining among the mellow notes of the water, from some far field the corncrake's brazen call, and made the gold ring stronger. These sounds, the pale moonlight, the night, and the idea of Muriel, possessed him to the exclusion of thought. Passion rendered him impassive, and he waited without impatience. Slowly pealing from the tower in Gourock, ten strokes told the hour. A crackling twig, a footstep, a rustle, and Muriel was beside him.

Nothing was said till she had recovered her breath; then her voice, timed unconsciously to the rippling accompaniment of the waves, whispered clear, 'When you had gone, my father locked me in my room. The thought of waiting-and-waiting here all night would soon have made me mad, so I got out by the window. I threw out a cushion, and then I was frightened. But after a little my courage came back again, and then I threw over two more, and dropped down quite soft. I don't know whether any one saw or heard me; but you wanted me, and I'm here. See, I tore my dress.'

He kissed her dress.

'You must not enter your father's house again,' he said.

Her breath came quick; she took his arm, and looked at him intently.

'Do you know your father?' he asked.

'He is difficult; but I am beginning to.'

'Then you will understand why his house is not for you.'

She had only a look with which to answer, and he did not think it satisfactory.

'Tell me,' he said, 'do you understand?'

'No; I do not. My father wants me to marry a stranger, but he cannot make me.'

'Then you do not know him. He has no scruples; he will do anything.'

'What can he have said to impress you so?'

'He said enough to show me he has no conscience, and that he looks on you as a mere puppet.'

Muriel felt as if the world were breaking up on all sides. What strange new things the day had brought forth; and, to crown them, flight from home seemed imminent! She pressed to her side Frank's arm, and with her disengaged hand smoothed the collar of his coat and fastened the top button, all the while looking wistfully at his set face. The ears of both were ringing with their own blood, or they would have heard a movement among the branches; for at that moment Lee reached the elm. His intention was to interrupt at once, and get back to the ravelled skein in the house; but the vision of the two lovers solaced his artistic sense; he was so near that he could hear their whispers. Shall not an artist take delight in his own work? Chance would help him, as it had done, manfully. He would watch this scene out. Surely he held the strings; and these, his daintiest puppets, he must see them play their best.

'You must come away with me,' said Frank hoarsely. 'See, I would have you what is called elope, and I am scrupulous. I do not know if such an action can be justified by our position even to ourselves. Your father has no scruples. Conceive what he will do.'

Two incidents flashed into Muriel's mind; the elopement of one former schoolmate, and the forced marriage of another; both ending in death by heartbreak of the young wives. She was angry at herself that these should have occurred to her. Frank and she!—they were apart from the world. Yet she whispered, 'You surely exaggerate.'

'No; I do not,' he said. 'Come with me, just now. We are in Scotland. I will marry you to-night—regularly, to-morrow. You needn't fear; I have plenty of money.'

'Frank!' she cried reproachfully, 'if I thought my marrying you depended on running off just now, I would go although you hadn't a penny.'

'It does, it does. Step on the wall, and I will help you down.'

This command, and the action which accompanied it, roused her. She had not fully realised the purpose that made his pleading so earnest, until he seized her quickly, and lifted her towards the wall.

Lee grasped his whip tightly, and was ready for a spring.

'Put me down,' said Muriel.

Frank hesitated for a moment. It came into his brain to profess a misunderstanding of her meaning, and lift her over; but looking in her eyes he blushed with shame at the imagination of such a deceit. When she was free she seated herself at the root of the tree, and clasped her knees, gazing at vacancy. She sat for a full minute. He did not interrupt her meditation. He scarcely thought that she had divined his momentary impulse. Nevertheless, he felt as if she had, and punished himself by remaining silent and apart. He watched her face. It was a sweet perplexity. He chafed to think that he could not resolve her difficulty.

At length her brow cleared. She rose and went to the wall. She looked up and down the road and over her shoulder enchantingly. Then she lifted her skirts over the wall and sat with her back to Frank. In a second she turned round, and dropped with a little laugh into the road. He sprang after her, and seized her hand. Lee approached the wall, but still kept himself concealed.

'Muriel!' Frank whispered breathlessly.

'Frank,' she said, giving him her hand, 'I will do what you think right. That's what I meant by coming over the wall—I am in your hands. But first I will tell you what I think. My father wishes me to marry his friend. That is all we know at present. If the time should come when I must either obey my father or fly with you, you know what I would do. But I do not see that that time can ever come.'

'Yes,' said he. 'But if your father should give you this alternative—either to marry his friend or remain single?'

'I was coming to that, although it seems too ridiculous to be likely. Well, we would elope.'

There was silence for several seconds. Unwittingly they had to accustom themselves to the changed environment, although the difference was slight. Their natures were so quickened, so responsive, that soon a perfect accord existed between them and the latticeless moonbeams, the wide, open night, and the undeadened music of the surges. They crossed the road in order to be wholly free of the shade of the elm, not thinking why they did so. Lee, on his knees behind the wall, watched them with glowing eyes.

At length Frank said, 'You are here; you are beautiful; you are hopeful; and you make me hopeful too. I have dreamt so long of having you that I cannot, with you beside me, imagine our not being married. But I force myself to remember your father's determined tone, his cold-blooded sophistries. I heard the worst, most insolent, most foul, most damnable——'

'Frank!'

'Most foolish talk fall from your father's lips about you, Muriel. It is horrible to talk to you in this way; but I tremble when I think of your being left to your father's tender mercies. Listen. I have challenged him to keep you from me, and he has accepted the challenge. I regret it now. He said that he would use every means; that he was always armed to the teeth; so I resolved at once to run away with you, and dared him. I have been rash—or should I save you in spite of yourself?'

She looked at the ground, working with both hands at the buttons of her dress. He had described her mental condition as well as his own. His presence had cast into the shade the recollection of her talk with Lee. The threat contained in what Lee had said about 'coming to the point and never returning to it' now assumed portentous shape in her fancy, quickened by Frank's forebodings; and the happy, trustful, resolved expression which her face had worn when she climbed over the wall gave place to one of wretched doubt.

Frank, watching her closely, would not take advantage of her wavering mood, and refrained from word or action. His whole endeavour had been to overcome her repugnance to an elopement; yet when it was shaken, he made no attempt to improve the occasion. He felt that to do so would be like striking a man when he is down. What he aimed at was to make her throw him the reins and be passive. This she had seemed to do when she went over the wall, but the surrender had not been absolute.

'I am puzzled,' she said hastily, knitting her brows at the moon. 'I cannot decide. I shall tell you how I am thinking, and then, perhaps, I shall find out what it is right to think. It is clearer to think aloud. Elopement! It is a bad, vulgar thing. It would be in all the papers—forgive me, love! I am thinking that way. I can't help it. People would joke about it as long as we lived. My father would never forgive me. Frank—Frank Hay! I love him, and he loves me. My father doesn't love me. Frank wants me to elope. What would it matter about newspapers and society when we were married? I am a foolish girl. It always comes round to this: would it be right just now? Could it ever be right? Here I am in the road. You must decide.'

This was spoken with extraordinary emphasis, and at a great rate of speed; and when it was done the trouble passed off her face. It settled on his. He pushed his hat from his forehead, thrust his hands into his pockets, confronting her, and said, 'I hoped for this, and intended to carry you off in triumph. Whatever withholds me, I cannot.'

Vacillation is not always the sign of a weak nature. The wind veers round the compass, and then the gale sets in steadily. Frank had never been on such a high sea of moral difficulty before. He had some crew of principles; but they were not able-bodied, having slept for the most part through the plain sailing of his life. When the storm came the drowsy helmsman, Conscience, started up rubbing his blinking eyes; and Will, the captain, had no order to give.

He climbed the wall, and held down his hands to Muriel. She put one foot in a little hole; he pulled her up; and they were again under the elm, Lee barely escaping discovery.

Now, just at the instant Frank gave Muriel his hands, and she clambered up the wall with the grace of a wild thing and the necessary free movements; just when her panting body was in his arms, and her breath upon his face, there came out of the south one long, gentle, trembling, warm sigh, bearing a burden of subtle odour from the half-reaped hay fields, and making the trees shiver with delight through all their happy branches, and the sap swell and trickle to the very tips of the downiest twigs. It was Summer kissing Nature in the night. Frank and Muriel were caught in the contagion. Passion whirled round their hearts that had been held by consciences alike inexperienced, and the poor helmsmen were overset. Their blood rattled along their veins like uncontrolled rudder-chains. He lifted her over; and, taking her in his arms again when he joined her in the road, started to carry her. They would be married that night.

A long shadow thrown suddenly across the road arrested him, and immediately a tall figure stood up in the moonlight. He set Muriel on her feet behind him, and faced Lee.

'Mr. Chartres!' he exclaimed hoarsely.

'You wished,' said Lee, handing him the riding whip, 'for an opportunity to horsewhip me.'

'Villain!' cried Frank savagely, seizing the whip. He raised it to strike. His rage was simply that of a foiled animal.

'Haven't you got over that bad habit of calling names yet?' said Lee with a smile, as he caught the hand that held the descending whip. Frank shifted it to the other hand, which Lee grasped as quickly. Thus Lee held by the wrist a hand of Frank's in each of his.

Muriel uttered a little scream and fell on her knees. She kept her eyes fixed on the whip. It jerked about overhead for a few seconds and fell to the ground. Then she looked at the men. Their arms were locked round each other. They staggered about and knocked against the wall. She heard them breathing hard. She held her own breath. She had scarcely begun to think what would be the upshot when Frank fell with a thud on his back, and Lee stood over him whip in hand.

'You have killed him!' she screamed, starting to her feet, and rushing to her prostrate lover.

'Hardly,' said Lee, throwing the whip away, rather ostentatiously, as he stepped aside to let Frank rise. He got up looking very unheroic; indeed, decidedly sheepish. Lee folded his arms, paler, if anything, than the other, and said, 'I won't ask you to try another fall. I think I am just twice as strong as you. I mean this to be a lesson. If you are wise, you will not attempt to struggle with me in anything.'

Frank stood with his eyes fixed on the ground; his self-esteem had fallen with his body; Muriel had seen him beaten.

Lee, resting a hand on Muriel's shoulder, and forcing her to stand beside him when she shrank away, said gaily, 'She is really a splendid girl, this daughter of mine. How handsome she looks just now! You must be chagrined horribly when you think that you almost had her. My dear boy, I pity you sincerely. I don't know exactly what course you should follow. It would be very striking, certainly, if you were to go off and drown yourself at once; but I don't think you'll do that. For myself I would prefer that you shouldn't. I like you too well, and hope that you will continue to play a part in our story. Perhaps you might take to drink. That's a good idea. Go in for dissipation; there's nothing like it for the cure of romance. Unworldly diseases need worldly remedies. And yet that's too common, especially with lady novelists. I believe you'll hit on some bright course of your own, for you're a capital collaborateur. I must thank you and Muriel for this scene. I've witnessed it all. Oh, you needn't be ashamed!' for Frank shut his eyes tightly, and Muriel hid her face in her hands. 'You're most delightful young people. The way you answered at once to that soft, warm gust charmed me, charmed me. I understand it all perfectly. I also am at one with nature. Well, good night. Come, Muriel.'

Taking her hand he moved toward the wall. She looked over her shoulder to catch a glance from Frank, but his eyes were still fixed on the ground, and he stood motionless. Quick as a fawn she leapt from Lee's side, and throwing her arms round Frank's neck, cried out loud in a tone mingled of anguish and pity and passion, 'I love you!' and he, reanimated by that shout, whispered as Lee snatched her away, 'I'll watch here all night.' That gave her new hope too. She would come to him by some means or other; and she felt so contented as Lee helped her over the wall, and led her in silence to the house, that she wondered at herself.

CHAPTER XI

CONCLUSION

It was nearly eleven o'clock. Lee, Briscoe, Miss Jane, Dempster and Muriel were all in the dining-room, and Dempster was making a speech. It will possibly never be known whether Miss Jane put him up to it or not; if she did she regretted it before he was half done.

'Ladies and gentlemen,' he began, with turgid tongue and desiccated throat, 'you are surprised that I should wish at this late hour to detain you with anything in the shape of a formal speech, however informal it may be.' The introductory sentence had been prepared. 'But,' he continued, staunching a wriggle, 'I—I have something to say. Mr. Chartres, I am neither a Communist nor a Nihilist'—this was to have been a side flourish, but out it came first—'still I would like to remark, in reference to a talk we had this afternoon, that I am of opinion that, if fortunes were things to be inherited by everybody, it might on the whole be better—eh—ah—or worse for society, taking into consideration the fact that wealth produces idleness, and idleness folly, and—eh—ah—sin, it might be better that most people should have to make their fortunes. Eh—ah—I am overwhelmed with a feeling such as one experiences when one gets something one didn't expect. Comfort, Mr. Chartres, is the greatest necessity of existence—I mean that to be comfortable is always of the greatest consequence, indeed, I may say, the very backbone—eh—ah—of comfort.'

Now there is never the remotest necessity for speech-making, at least in private, although it is daily perpetrated, and unfailingly by wholly incompetent parties. It is like singing in this respect; only those who cannot care to perform. Human nature will never get past it; for there is a law which ordains that whatever one is unfit for must be attempted, especially out of season. What one can't do is the all-important thing. So Dempster reeled on, undeterred by the blank looks of his auditors, and an ominous sparkle in Miss Jane's eye—his body a mere thoroughfare of uninterrupted transmigration for the spirits of all things that crawl and squirm and twist and wriggle.

'And I am now, I am happy to say, exceedingly comfortable. After Muriel refused me I was like a ship in a storm, and so I put into the first port—eh—ah—I mean that I have found a comfortable haven, and I am sure Jane will make a very good wife.'

Amazement stared from every eye, including Miss Jane's. She tried to simper in a dignified manner—but what was the man saying?

'She is like old wine—eh—ah'—he felt Miss Jane's eyes scorching him like burning-glasses. 'The difference between our ages—eh—ah——' He was now perspiring freely. 'The disadvantage of marrying a girl like Muriel is, that when she grows old'—he made a little halt here, but he was too far gone to draw back; over he went, head first—'when she grows old one would miss her beauty. The great advantage is that one can never miss what has never been there, and—I'll not be interrupted!' mopping his head, and gyrating fiercely; but not daring to meet again Miss Jane's eye, one full glance of which had been more than enough.

'There's nobody interrupting you, my dear Mr. Dempster,' said Lee. 'But is it true that you are going to marry my sister?'

'It is—I am!' defiantly, as if he were challenging himself to take so much as one step in an opposite direction.

'I'm very glad. An episode of this kind is refreshing. So unlikely too! One daren't have introduced it into written fiction; but here it has cropped up most beautifully in our little creation. Really, I am much obliged to you both. Now you must allow me to go upstairs and attend to the matters there.'

As soon as Lee had reached the house with Muriel he had gone straight to the room in which Henry Chartres lay; but when he was about to enter, a swift descending step on the stair caught his ear, and drew him away just in time to intercept Briscoe, who had finally determined that, wherever he might go, he must leave Snell House that night. Lee peremptorily bade him stay, or he would accuse him of robbery, and send in pursuit; and Briscoe was forced to submit. Lee had been about to ascend the stair again, when Dempster importunately demanded his presence in the dining-room. The latter having made his remarkable communication, Lee intended to arrange with Briscoe some definite plan of action; but another delay took place.

On opening the door of the dining-room, Lee was met by Clacher, whom everybody had forgotten.

'Good evening,' said Clacher, doing it 'Englified,' and walking into the room. His face was streaming with perspiration; his eyes were wild with drink and insanity; his hair hung in wisps about his face.

'Ladies and gentlemen, I am Robert Chartres,' he said. He had remembered what he wanted to do 'Englified.'

'I am bonnie Prince Charlie too,' he added, after a pause. 'I don't understand it. I'm afraid I'm mad but I'm not a fool. I am Robert Chartres.'

Everybody looked at Lee.

He said, 'I don't remember being so intensely interested in my life. How can you possibly hope to succeed in this imposture, Clacher?'

'You're an imposture,' cried Clacher fiercely, staggering a little. 'I'm mad, but I'm no jist a fule, an' naebody daur harm me. Ach!' he hissed, grinding his teeth and shaking his wild hair, enraged at himself for failing to do it 'Englified.' 'I am Robert Chartres,' he shouted, throwing back his head. 'The estate's entailed, and it's mine. I'm bonnie Prince Charlie, too,' he added, more quietly.

'Take a seat,' said Lee. 'Let us all sit down again.'

Clacher stumbled into a chair. Miss Jane forgave Dempster with her eyes, and they sat on a couch together. Muriel stood beside a window with one hand wrapped in the curtain. Briscoe sat opposite Lee, who threw himself back on a large chair on one side of the fireplace. Clacher's chair was against the wall, not far from the door.

'Jane,' said Lee, 'I find no resemblance between this gentleman and Robert. Do you?'

'Not the slightest,' said Miss Jane.

'Do yon, Muriel?'

'None.'

'Well, friend,' said Lee, turning to Clacher. 'What have you to say, now?'

'I am Robert Chartres.'

'But none of us recognise you. Recall yourself to our memories in some way.'

'Oh, I'm bonnie Prince Charlie too.'

'That only indicates that you are mad; and a very ordinary madness it is. I am sure there are two or three bonnie Prince Charlies in every lunatic asylum in Scotland.'

'I'm mad, an' naebody daur harm me,' growled Clacher.

'You remember Robert's escapade when he was a boy, Henry?' said Miss Jane.

'To which do you refer? There were so many,' said Lee.

'Oh, not so very many,' said Miss Jane. 'I mean the Inverkip Glen affair.'

'I can't say I do remember it.'

'Oh, you must. You weren't here at the time; but you knew all about it.'

Lee sat up, and swiftly changed his look of anxiety into a far-reaching glance at the past.

'Ah, yes!' he said, dropping back in his chair again.

'Clacher must have heard about it,' said Miss Jane.

'I shouldn't wonder,' said Lee. 'Clacher, do you know about the Inverkip Glen affair?'

'Of course. I'm Robert Chartres. I'm Clacher too, and Bonnie Prince Charlie. I don't know how.'

'Then,' said Lee, 'just tell us about it. Your acquaintance with it may be evidence of your identity.'

'The Inverkip Glen business?' said Clacher. 'A'body kens that. Damn!' he growled at the Scotch.

'Let us see, now,' said Lee. 'Have you any details that could only be known to Robert and his family?'

'Inverkip Glen,' said Clacher. 'When I was fourteen or thereabouts, I went away wi' a wheen laddies an' hid in it for twa-three days. I ca'ed mysel' Prince Charlie, an' the ithers wis cheeftans—Lochiel an' Glengarry, ye ken. We fought the servants that wis sent tae bring us hame, an' they had tae send the polis tae fetch us.'

This was spoken very haltingly, and ended with a savage oath at his own inability to speak correctly.

'He could have learned all that in the village,' said Miss Jane.

Lee rose, leant gracefully against the mantelpiece, and addressed Clacher.

'Clacher,' he said, 'you have unwittingly undertaken a work of art, and for that you deserve high commendation. You have aspired; you have done your best. That is sufficient. Success is the only failure. A compassable aim is an inferior one. Ideals cease to be when realised. Better succeed in a constant endeavour after the highest, than fail in aspiration to achieve a result as splendid as any which history records. These platitudes are not by any means beside the question, although you don't understand them.'

Here Lee shifted from his easy pose, and stood firmly on his feet.

'Whatever besides madness,' he continued, 'may have led you to attempt this imposture, is no concern of mine. I am only sorry for your sake and my own that you cannot continue it further. Variety, if not the soul, is certainly the body of fiction. I hope that, although you must go out of our story shortly, at least in your present capacity, you, or some one else in your sphere of life, may be enmeshed in this web of circumstance which I help fate to weave. My brother Robert is at present upstairs. He arrived here this evening.'

Lee looked at all his auditors severally, thoroughly enjoying the effect of this extraordinary news.

'O dear! dear!' cried Clacher weakly, tedding his hair and fidgeting on his seat. 'Naebody daur harm me, I'm mad.'

'Set your mind at rest, Clacher. Nobody will attempt to harm you.'

'Jane,' he continued, 'it was our unfortunate brother whom we carried upstairs this evening. The woman was his wife.'

Briscoe gasped; but the practical novelist proceeded, smiling, and proud of his ingenuity.

'He has been going by the name of Lee, Maxwell Lee,' he said, staring down Briscoe; 'and makes a scanty living by his pen. His wife is a noble woman, and will not admit his madness; but that he is mad no one else can have any doubt, because the poor fellow imagines that he is me. I will tell you his whole history tomorrow, as far as I know it. I hadn't the remotest idea he was in Scotland until he appeared to-night——'

The droning of a bagpipe not far off, a strange sound at that time of night and in the neighbourhood, interrupted him. A very unskilful attempt at a pibroch succeeded, and as the playing grew more distinct it was evident that the performer approached the house. Muriel raised the window-sash, and the tuneless screaming ceased. Hesitating steps on the gravel were then heard. They stopped opposite the window, and a high, cracked male voice quavered out the first verse of Glen's pathetic ballad, 'Wae's me for Prince Charlie':—

> 'A wee bird cam tae oor ha' door,
> He warbl't sweet an' clearly;
> An' aye the o'ercome o' his sang
> Was "Wae's me for Prince Charlie."
> O! when I heard the bonnie, bonnie bird,
> The tears came drappin' rarely;
> I took my bonnet off my head,
> For well I lo'ed Prince Charlie!'

The voice broke entirely at the last line. Said Lee, 'We'll bring this minstrel in,' and left the room. In a few seconds he returned accompanied by a strange figure. It was that of an old man dressed in a ragged Highland costume. His kilt was of the Stuart tartan. His black jacket had been garnished with brass buttons; but of them only a few hung here and there, withered and mouldy; and numerous little tufts of thread on pocket-lids and cuffs and breast showed whence their companions had been shed. His sporran was half-denuded of hair. His hose were holed, and the uppers were parting company with the soles of his shoes. A black feather adorned in a very broken-backed manner his Glengarry bonnet. His pipes he had left in the hall.

There was nothing remarkable in the dress. Such are to be seen any day in the Trongate of Glasgow, the Canongate of Edinburgh, at fairs, or wherever the wandering piper may turn a penny. It was the bearing of the wearer and the cast of his countenance which commanded attention. As he entered the room he threw back his head, inclining it a little to the left side; his dim grey eyes lightened fitfully, and his gait had something of majesty. He advanced slowly, but without hesitation, and took the seat Lee had vacated.

Of all those in the room Clacher's face indicated the greatest interest.

'Friends,' said the newcomer, keeping on his bonnet, and shaking back his long grey hair, which hung almost to his shoulders, 'I can trust you. "Nowhere beats the heart so kindly as beneath the tartan plaid." You haven't the tartans on, and that is right, for they might betray you. There's a law against the tartan. I wear it in defiance of the law.'

'Wha are ye, man?' cried Clacher, his face undergoing a sudden illumination.

'Do you not know me?' said the stranger. 'You will be true. It is a great sum. Ten thousand pounds. All my own friends have forgotten me. It is strange, strange. I am changed, I know. I am Bonnie Prince Charlie.'

'Ha, ha!' screamed Clacher, 'ha, ha, ha!'

'Two of them,' whispered Dempster to himself, rigid with amazement.

'You astonish me,' said Lee with perfect composure.

'It is sad, I know. I sleep in the woods, and visit the towns at night. My home is in the bracken. I remember I lived here in 'forty-five. I thought I would revisit the old place to-night. Is not this Scone Palace?'

'No; this is Snell House.'

'Ah! I lived there too, once. But can you tell me this. Why do they accuse me of unfaithfulness? "Flora, when thou wert beside me!" Oh, her eyes were warm and mild like the summer, and her voice made me weep. It is shameful what they say about me. I never loved another.'

Clacher, looking absolutely hideous in his excitement, rushed from his chair, oversetting a small table, and planting himself firmly before the wondering piper, shouted, 'You are Bonnie Prince Charlie?'

'I am. Do me no harm.'

'Then you are Robert Chartres, and you did not commit suicide.'

'I am hungry,' said the Prince.

Clacher pulled from his breast-pocket the crumpled letter he had studied so devoutly in the library, and handing it to Miss Jane, cried: 'It's a' up noo'. I took that letter frae Maister Willum Chartres's pooch whan I fand his corp'. Read it, an' ye'll ken my plot. Gosh, it was a mad yin! Oh, I'm no jist a fule! Naebody daur harm me. An' you, ye scoon'erel,' he screamed, springing behind Lee, and pinning his arms to his body with a hug like a bear's, 'ye're mad, ye're mad. I've turn't the tables on ye, I'm thinking.'

Lee struggled strongly; but Briscoe came to Clacher's help.

'Peter!' exclaimed Lee.

'It's all up, as Clacher says. Every man for himself,' muttered Briscoe. But he wouldn't look Lee in the face.

'You've spoiled a great scene, Peter,' was all Lee said.

'And who is the man upstairs?' asked Muriel, advancing from the window.

'You'll get the key of the bedroom in which he is in this pocket,' said Briscoe, indicating by an uncouth gesture a pocket in his coat, as he did not wish to release his hold on Lee.

Muriel took the key and left the room.

Miss Jane read and re-read the letter given her by Clacher, and was still considering it when Muriel returned with her father. He was not long awake, and had to be supported by his daughter. Miss Jane recognised him at once and kissed his cheek. There was no exclaiming. When they came out of it they would know from their exhaustion how excited they had been. The tears stood in Muriel's eyes, and her face was very pale, but serenity marked every lineament.

'Where is Mrs. Lee?' asked Henry Chartres when he had got seated.

At that moment Caroline entered the room. She had remained in the bedroom Lee had appropriated, afraid lest her interference might precipitate some rash act on the part of her husband or her brother; but the bagpipes, the singing, the opening and shutting of doors, and the loud voices downstairs intimated a crisis of some kind, and she had concluded at last to have a share in it, hoping to prevent disaster to her husband, as she judged from the noise that his control of circumstances had come to an end. As Caroline entered, the two gardeners and the coachman appeared at the door, Muriel having sent for them at her father's request.

Muriel looked at Mrs. Lee for a second or two as if debating some question with herself, and then noiselessly left the room. She couldn't keep Frank waiting any longer.

'Maxwell Lee,' said Henry Chartres, 'for your wife's sake you go scot free. She has told me all about you. As for you, Peter Briscoe, your present action shows what you are. Take him and duck him well in the horse-pond.'

The coachman and the gardeners, nothing loath, approached Briscoe; but Lee, having regained his liberty, put himself before his brother-in-law in an attitude of defence.

'I beg you, sir, not to insist on this,' he said in a passion of intercession; 'it is mere revenge. I entreat you.'

'But he betrayed you,' said Chartres.

'Well, I suppose the world puts it that way. But he merely acted independently and without due consideration. That has been the fault of this work all along: the principal collaborateurs have been too frequently out of harmony. Since he has chosen to bring our story to a sudden end in this way, I have no right to complain. Do not damage your character for magnanimity which these events have developed so remarkably—a result very gratifying to me—by a petty revenge on my brother-in-law.'

Chartres signed to the servants to retire. 'You are a strange man,' he said.

'Miss Chartres,' said Lee, 'in token that you cherish no deep-rooted feeling against me, will you oblige me by reading that letter?'

Miss Jane looked at her brother; he assented, and she read:—

'My dear William,—You will be astonished, not very agreeably, I am afraid, to learn that I am still in the land of the living. I have been in a state of abject poverty for years. I will not trouble you with the particulars of my wretched career. I have burnt up my stomach with drink. Insanity has addled my brain. I am a beggar, and go about the country—I am ashamed to say it for your sake—playing the bagpipes. In my mad fits I have repeatedly tried to commit suicide. At present I am quite sane; the only difficulty I have is to reconcile my being Robert Chartres with the fact that I am also Bonnie Prince Charlie. I write this in London; and I am going to start at once and at last to try and come to you. It would be better to kill myself; but I am too great a coward when I am sane. I want to enjoy comfort once more before I die. If I do not reach you within a month after this letter, I think you may conclude that I am dead.

'I am, your brother,

'Robert Chartres.'

All eyes turned on the writer of the letter. He was fast asleep in his chair, smiling like a child.

'Briscoe,' said Lee, you recognised and submitted to the *deus ex machina* at once. I would have fought longer, and might yet have conquered. I am sorry the conclusion is so inartistic, so improbable. There is nothing more absurd than reality. Clacher, my fine fellow, you played a bold game; as the attempt of a mad rascal it was very fair. What a lot of mad people there are! How small the world is! Ah!' he cried, as Frank and Muriel entered, 'my good lovers! I believe you are even now thanking me for my opposition.'

'Who is this young gentleman?' asked Mr. Chartres.

'Oh! I found him at the north wall; I knew he would be there,' said Muriel, radiant, and scarcely knowing what she said.

'Do you frequently find young gentlemen and bring them here in this way?'

'Oh, papa! His name is Frank Hay, and we are going to be married.'

'I have never seen your like, Muriel,' said Lee, leaving the room. Briscoe followed him, bestowing a surly nod on Dempster. But Caroline before she went timidly kissed the hand of the injured man.

THE END